THE WRONG GIRL &
OTHER WARNINGS

PRAISE FOR ANGELA SLATTER'S SHORT STORIES

'Angela Slatter's stories are enviably original, and told in prose as stylish as it's precise. Not just disturbing but often touching, her work enriches and revives the tale of terror.' ~ **Ramsey Campbell**, author of *The Doll Who Ate His Mother, The Hungry Moon*, and *Told by the Dead*

'Angela Slatter is one of the treasures of current horror fiction. Her work is darkly magical, lyrical, and beautiful, and I can't recommend it highly enough.' ~ **Alison Littlewood**, author of *A Cold Season, The Unquiet House, A Cold Silence, The Path of Needles*

'Angela Slatter is an international treasure. She blends horror, fantasy, and fairy tale to create something entirely fresh, but which feels too like the nightmares half-forgotten when you were a child.' ~ **Robert Shearman**, author of *Love Songs for the Shy and Cynical, Remember Why You Fear Me*, and *They Do the Same Things Different There*

'Angela Slatter's wonderful collection is filled with tales of gruelling horror and shiver-inducing dread, often swathed in shades of the darkest humour. You won't want it to end.' ~ **Tim Lebbon**, author of *The Silence* and *The Hunt*

THE WRONG GIRL & OTHER WARNINGS

ANGELA SLATTER

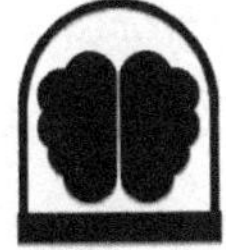

Brain Jar Press
PO Box 6687
Upper Mt Gravatt, QLD, 4122
Australia
www.BrainJarPress.com

Copyright © 2023 by Angela Slatter. Page 175 constitutes an extension of this copyright page.

The moral right of Angela Slatter to be identified as the author of this work has been asserted.

All rights reserved. No part of this book may be reproduced in any form or by any electronic or mechanical means, including information storage and retrieval systems, without written permission from the author, except for the use of brief quotations in a book review.

Cover design by Peter Ball
Cover Image: *little girl and the witch looking each other in a forest*, Tithi Luadthong/Shutterstock.

ISBN: 978-1-922479-60-0 (Ebook) | 978-1-922479-61-7 (Paperback)

CONTENTS

SAME TIME NEXT YEAR

It's just gone dusk, when the day bruises blue, and Cindy sits on the tomb, one of those big old ones shaped from grey granite into a box, about four feet high by six long by two wide; it's not hers. She's wearing a black leather jacket she got from god-knows-where and she's drinking a beer. It's got the word 'craft' on its label, which is pink, like no beer bottle she'd ever seen in her life. It tastes kinda weird, not like she remembers. Then again, she's not really tasting it, is she?

Hell, it was free, set like an offering on a grave with a bunch of wildflowers that were probably wilting even before they got left, so no complaints. And then again, it's not like the beer does anything but pour through her, what with ghosts lacking in solidity and all. It's just waterfalling from her lips, inside her throat, outside her neck, down her front, through her lap, and pattering onto the slab beneath her spectral butt.

Cindy shrugs off the leather jacket, drapes it on the tomb; it might be here when she gets back, it might not. Things disappear and reappear in the cemetery with surprising regularity. So does she, sometimes. If it was just stuff, just things, she'd suppose *Kids*, like an old lady. Kids daring each other to jump the rusty iron fence and run through, teens trying for the high of making love amongst the dead ('coming while you're going,' someone used to say yet she cannot remember who for the life or death of her). But who else except her could pick up this thing that's not really made of leather, not anymore, just wishes and cobwebs and bad dreams? Maybe a memory or two, although not ones she can recall. Besides, not many come out here nowadays, none but those who've got no choice.

It's not like she needs it against the cold or anything. Beneath the jacket she's wearing a dress, the dress she woke in, the lavender chiffon whisper of a thing that's almost a nightgown, maybe a prom dress. She wonders, oh yes she does, where she was going and what she was doing when she died, but that seems to have been wiped away with her passing.

Passing.

Stupid word. Dying, gone, rotted, decayed.

Dead.

She's sure as shit she never owned anything like this in life. There are splinters and shards of before she woke here. Cracks and fractures and fragments of a rundown house, small squalling siblings (their number is never fixed), a woman who yelled and a man who yelled louder still. Maybe there was some school, too, but she can't quite lay heavy hold on those thoughts. But there must have been, if she's dressed for a prom, right? Junior or senior? Who knows?

She shivers, a human action remembered, not felt. She looks down, notices some dark spots on the skirt. She waves a hand across them and they disappear: either covered or disintegrated, she doesn't really know. The things she can do she doesn't really understand, but wishes she'd been able to do them in life, might have made living a damned sight easier. Whatever her life was then it doesn't feel easy, not in the broken recollections that float in her head. Whatever comes back to her has no rhyme or reason.

But now, *right now*, she can feel the weight coming upon her—one night, one night a year—she should have waited to drink the beer. How could she forget that? Cindy reaches out and touches the jacket: yes, it feels different now, weighty. The scent of it is dead and dusty, animal and musky. Old, old, old. She pushes herself away from the tomb, takes steps that are at first tiny, then grow longer, grander as she feels her own heft upon the earth. The grass is dry, this time of year, a fire risk, but it's not as if that bothers her or anyone else here. The little chapel by the half-empty pond is painted red and white like a barn; half the roof's caved in. No one tends to anything anymore. The paths are overgrown, the hedges are scrappy, the trees thin-limbed, their leafy cover sparse against the darkening sky; just enough to keep the light of the incipient stars at bay. Clouds cover the moon but she doesn't need light to see by.

The rows of the cemetery aren't especially orderly, and the headstones ... many of them have a lean to them, and layers of moss, names and dates worn away. She can't remember where the bones of her lie, not anymore, if she ever knew.

When she begins to *thicken*, some of the memories come back, but not that one, never that one. It makes her think that maybe she wasn't ever properly interred. *Interred*. What a word. Fancy way of saying *planted*.

Cindy.

The last boy called her that. She doesn't know what function she was fulfilling for him, only knows he called her that as he put his hands around her throat, pushed himself into her—there's just one night a year she can be solid. He sounded so angry as he said the name, even angrier when she began to laugh despite the choking pressure of his big hands. Not so angry when she dissolved beneath him, left him with cock rapidly softening, mouth slack and fingers empty.

He got up, though, got up and ran. She just floated along behind, dead breath at his shoulder, a purplish mist. She stayed with him until he ran into an oak tree. He'd put his head down, running like he was heading towards a touchdown, so when he hit the trunk it was at just the right angle to fracture his neck. Not enough to kill him, though; she watched him flop back on the grass and lie still. His gaze shifted—the only thing that could move, she guessed—and he watched her with concentrated terror. How quickly things changed! She watched him in turn for a while, grinning like a loon, then settled on his broad chest, put one hand—suddenly solid, suddenly heavy, this one night—onto his throat and began to squeeze.

He took a while to die. Four minutes, isn't it, to strangulation? She was sure she'd read that somewhere. She'd touched her own throat with her free hand; stroked the non-flesh, felt it give, pushed her fingers through it, just a little— not *entirely* solid, then—and felt creeped out. She'd pulled her fingers away. She wanted to tell him that she was angry too; everybody was angry even if not everyone could recall the why of it, but what was he going to do with that knowledge?

At the end of those four minutes, though, he was gone. Gone. The core of him, the spirit, the equivalent of the whatever-of-Cindy-that-remained-behind: his *went*. She never saw him again, neither hide nor ectoplasmic hair. And Lordy, wasn't that so unfair? That he got to disappear and she had to hang around here like *she*'d done something bad? Stuck forever in detention after school.

Cindy.

She can't even remember her own name, but she remembers that one.

It's as good as any.

They'll be coming soon. It's about time. That's right, she thinks, remembering now, pieces and remnants.

Friday night was always dance night.

They all used to come out here, the kids, drunk and high, brave as crazed 'coons. They didn't think too much at all, just following primal urges, dark desires and yearnings with no consideration of whether getting what they wanted was a good idea. She's pretty sure she didn't get anything good for her, but the memories are still not there, not properly. It's just flickering screens like a ruined film, a flipbook of figures: her, two boys, a case of beer. She doesn't want to look, she decides.

The clouds shift and the moon shows her own face, just a sliver, just a hint.

Cindy shakes her head; doesn't see a lot of folk here nowadays, though. None, really, to be precise. Too far outside of town, there are other places, better places, more comfortable for getting into trouble. Sometimes boys and girls used to come though—that boy who ran into the tree, and gave her a name, and who she'd have left alone if he'd not behaved so badly, but he'd wandered in that night, that one night, and well ... there you go. She didn't encounter too many girls once upon a time, but behaviours changed, oh yes they did, and for a while young women used to hide out, smoke, drink, what-have-you. Cindy listened a lot when they talked, curious and bemused. Apparently equality meant behaving as badly as men, rather than setting an expectation that they behave better. But she'd never bothered the girls; figured they'd got enough shit to deal with on their own without her adding to matters. Cindy shakes her head; the only true equality they've got is death.

Lordy, Lordy, when did she become a philosopher?

About ten years after you died, says a voice in her head, *ten years of sitting alone in a bone orchard talking to yourself.*

'there's no one else around,' she says aloud. But even then, she's not quite sure when it was or how long she's been around.

The air's cool on her skin now and Cindy enjoys the sensation. There are no noises in the night, but she's here so seldom, her memory's so thin, that it doesn't really strike her, the lack of owl hoots, possums, foxes, wild cats and the like. Not even an insect, not a katydid singing. Nothing, just her bare feet on dried grass, *crunch, crunch, crunch*.

So the voices come clear through air that's uncontaminated by other sound, though they're low murmurs, that tone boys have before their voices settle proper. Cindy sees them before they see her.

Two boys. Youths. Young men, really, not quite tall and their limbs still gangly like they don't quite know what to do with their bits and pieces. Slicked back hair, one head black, the other blond, both with cigarettes in overly-large hands. Furtive looks beneath beetle-brows, and confused. Uncertain, as if they don't know how they got here. Familiar, familiar, familiar.

Then they see her and stare. Cindy keeps her pace steady, dignified; the pace of a girl going to her prom, so the lavender mist of skirt swirls around her. She clasps her hands in front at first, but it feels wrong, so she swings them, slaps them into the small of her back and suddenly looks like a general on parade. She lifts her chin, too, juts it forward and the moon spills from behind the last cloud to show Cindy's face to the young men.

Whatever they see, they crack.

Cigarettes are tossed to the ground, bounce with tiny red flares on the dry grass, but Cindy walks over the greedy flames, snuffs them before they can get a hold. She feels the burns as a tickle, a lick, and continues on. She doesn't quicken at all, but somehow they can't pull away from her. Maybe it's all the headstones they're dodging around and between, as if they don't want to disrespect the dead by thudding over them. Cindy has no such qualms, she puts her feet down where she will.

'Hello, boys,' she calls, but they offer no answer, although she thinks perhaps she hears a whimper. Maybe that's just wishful thinking.

They hurdle the rusty iron fence like track stars. They breach a boundary she cannot, no matter how much she's tried or how often over the years. They slip and slide and tumble down into the dusty ditch by the side of the road that hardly sees any traffic, then scramble up the other incline. Both break onto the asphalt like birds loosed, like they're hitting the tape at the end of a running track: arms up, chests out, heads tipped back.

The car comes out of nowhere.

There's no sound, at least not until the last moment, when the engine roars just before it hits. And it hits them both at the same time. She thinks neither of them have their feet on the ground, they're still in flight, still in motion, still flying through the air with the greatest of ease.

Cindy's hands go to her throat, delighted shock, gleeful awe, awful glee.

Boys and vehicle—a turquoise and white Chevrolet Bel Air with its top up—burst.

One moment, they are themselves. The next they're stardust and particles, strangely wet-looking, a red fleck beneath the moon as the confetti of them drifts down to the road's surface.

'Happy anniversary. Same time next year, assholes,' she says and as soon as the words are out she begins to forget they were ever there. She loses her weight, her density. The dress turns to the consistency of candy floss once again. She can't see the jacket anymore, but maybe she's wandered too far from it. She feels lighter, lighter, lighter, she is moonlight and dust and a bitter breath on the night breeze.

Damn but there was something she wishes she could remember ...

WIDOWS' WALK

The house on Carter Lane—Second Empire style, mansard roof with dormers, a tower, patterned shingles, deep eaves and elaborately pedimented windows, all painted in shades of white, cappuccino, and deepest chocolate—is home to four widows between the ages of fifty-nine and eighty-two.

Once only Martha lived there but the others gradually shifted into it as husbands shuffled off mortal coils, either naturally or otherwise. Some remodelling has been done and now each has her own suite on the second floor: large bedroom, bathroom, sitting room and tiny study nook with a desk and chair; there's a guest room, too, just in case. Downstairs, there's a kitchen, library and parlour, where the Widows meet when they've a mind, for meals and discussions of various matters. Every morning the first to rise—invariably Sarah, the oldest, whose bladder won't let her rest past five—taps on the others' doors to make sure no one's died in the dark watches.

Rumour in Mercy's Brook says that this task might well be performed by any of the three cats (only one of which is black) that've taken up residence with the old women, for as all know, both felines and aged females are equally suspect. Although anyone who knows anything about cats also knows they are ultimately self-interested and won't trouble themselves to check on anyone's health unless it's likely to affect their own feeding.

Despite the fact they're far from the coast, there's a widow's walk on the roof—which gives the house its unofficial name—but only Eugenie is inclined to use it. The youngest, she's surest of her feet and she goes up there to smoke, sometimes blue-fumed cheroots, sometimes something sweeter to dull the pain of her arthritic fingers. Virginia prefers to sit inside the tower room and stare out the windows on the days when her inclinations lean that way, overlooking the garden, watching it grow, watching the foxes that visit. Sarah spends her time in the library, mostly, reading and writing down the things she doesn't want lost to the world when she dies. Martha's favourite spot is the garden, actually being *in* it, digging and planting, growing and cultivating things for use in the kitchen and her apothecary experiments.

They rub along, the Widows, rather better than might be expected given their differing personalities and interests, and Eugenie's tendency to swear mightily at the drop of a hat, which often offends Martha's delicate sensibilities. She's grown adept at pursing her mouth to communicate disapproval, which inevitably brings 'don't you give me fucking lips of string, Martha Foster!' shouted so loudly it can be heard from the street. Yet they'll all admit quite freely that living with each other requires less effort than living with their husbands ever did, and when matters boil over as they occasionally must, things simply settle back into a comfortable rhythm with no residual resentment or bitterness.

They're all born and bred in Mercy's Brook, the Widows,

which isn't such a bad place, and no one actively points fingers and calls 'Witch!' when they see the old women doing their groceries or taking tea at Abigail Hobbs' bookstore and café (although those of German extraction occasionally whisper *hexen* behind their cupped palms). No children throw stones at the pristine windows that Martha pays a local lad to clean fortnightly, nor do they run up to ring the bell and bolt away; then again, that might have something to do with a fear that the black-painted gate might somehow lock itself at an inopportune moment. But Virginia has noticed with a certain glee that folk do sometimes cross the road when they walk past; Martha says it's so they can see the glory of the house better, not because they're afraid. Sarah and Eugenie don't bother to contradict her, though they roll their eyes something fierce.

It's early, this morning, just gone half-past five, and the light is barely scraping the sky. The temperatures are beginning to dip and soon the leaves will be on the turn from green to orange-flame, as if the trees are burning themselves to stay warm. All the Widows are awake, three in the kitchen: two gathered around the coffee pot, one slicing the bread that's fresh out of the bread-maker; no lights are on, though, not today. Virginia's still upstairs, in the unlit tower room, which is empty but for the armchair she likes, a footstool and a small polished wooden side table where she can rest her teacup in the afternoon.

When she calls, they can hear her voice quite clearly for it carries unnaturally well along the hallway and down the stairs. *The place has always had good acoustics*, Martha's said before with a shrug.

'Girl's out there again.'

Eugenie, Martha and Sarah share a knowing glance and grin. Eugenie takes a sip of her coffee then sets the mug on the counter. She opens the door to the root cellar, making sure to flick on the powerful lights that illuminate the subterranean room like a ship at sea—oh, she'll turn it off as soon as she's in place. Then her slipper-clad feet take the path downward.

Chelsea Margaret Bloom, mindful of the warnings she's heard about exits that snap shut at inopportune moments, has propped her bicycle in the gap between gate and fence. It's still quite dark, and although she's done this very same thing five days in a row without consequence, she's not entirely confident.

The streetlight outside Widows' Walk never works for the Widows find it annoying, and no number of repairmen from the local power company have managed to fix it for any great length of time. Eventually, the neighbours gave up reporting it. The Widows, strong believers in positive reinforcement, sent everyone in Carter Lane boxes of homemade cookies; some were eaten and declared wondrous and almost as good as those served in Abigail Hobbes' café (in fact, they were identical, the Widows being Abi's supplier), but others sent straight to the bin, for some will always believe that no good gift comes from the hands of witches.

So, Chelsea's at least reassured by the remaining darkness, by the fact she knows she only requires a few moments to do what she needs to, and so is perhaps a little less attentive than she's been on previous occasions. She doesn't notice that the bushes of sneezeweed with their flowers of orange and yellow have been pruned back somewhat, that the tiny basement window level with the garden bed is ajar, or that a shadow moves behind its glass. It's still quite gloomy, after all, and she's paying more attention to the bigger windows for some gleam that will show her the Widows are awake.

There's nothing.

Chelsea does what she's done the better part of the last week: takes a deep breath and begins to tiptoe along the cobbled path in her worn sneakers, and tries not to think about how hungry she is, hopes that her stomach won't betray her by growling (*Honestly, how loud could it be?*). She tries not to think about the tales they tell at school of boys who've set out to explore Widows' Walk and disappeared, only to be found a few days later, wandering in the woods, with no memory of where they've been—although no one can ever give the names of those boys, and it's not as if Sheriff Taylor has ever been reported as looking for them. Or the stories of the girls who've gone to live in that house and come out changed, moving away from Mercy's Brook, or staying; she tries not to think of that option with longing. Chelsea shakes her head, eyes her prize.

Two milk bottles on the top step: full cream with silver-blue caps on top. The milkman has already been, left the daily order. Chelsea only takes one, just one, she's not greedy. Heck, she'd only take half if she could, but it seems kind of rude to leave a half-empty bottle of milk ... it's not like folk are going to drink the leftovers, right? Who knows what might have been done to it?

Besides, it tides her over, that whole bottle, so she's only a little hungry by the end of the day, and when she gets home ... well, generally, her mother has roused herself to get some groceries, make pancakes, or to bring something home from the café where she gets a few shifts a week because Miz Hobbes is kind. But lately Ellie's been more distracted than usual ...

Chelsea creeps closer; hard to believe that this is the easiest house to steal from, but there you go: it's on her route to school, the neighbours aren't too near, and Chelsea's got an idea in her head that old folks sleep more than they actually do. She thinks, for a second, she hears something: a scrape, a creak, a crack, and she freezes. But though she freezes forever—

or maybe only fifteen seconds—nothing else stirs. She hears a crow caw, and decides that must have been it, a fat crow on a branch too thin. Chelsea keeps going; she makes it to the top of the path, does what she always does, which is to not go up the stairs, lest she be too visible from the glass-panelled doors, but rather steps to the side, half-in-half-out of the garden, the sneezeweed brushing her scrawny legs. She shuffles so her stance is solid, then leans forward, and her stick-fingers are reaching for the nearest bottle, slowly, slowly ...

... when a hand grabs her ankle, and she almost pees herself.

She certainly lets out a god-awful shriek that conjures a laugh, only a little malicious, from the cellar window, and activity at front entrance, where two old women swarm down to her, embroidered dressing gowns flapping like cloaks, like wings. When it's sure she's in the crones' custody, the hand around her ankle lets go, the laughter gets softer as its owner moves away from the window, and Chelsea is bodily lifted up the stairs and into the house, astonished, in the beats between her fear, at how strong the Widows are.

'She's too young for coffee, really.' Martha fusses with more slices of toast.

'Well, hot chocolate will send her to sleep, then how will the girl fuc—function at school?' Eugenie seems to be mindful of keeping her language under control, given their company.

'You could give her tea?' ventures Virginia. She's quelled by the looks of the other Widows.

'I like coffee just fine,' says Chelsea in a small voice. These are certainly the most peculiar witches ... unless this is some sort of a Gingerbread House situation and they're trying to fatten her up. She doesn't mind, the bread and jams are the best she's ever had. The first proper breakfast she's had in the longest time.

'Make it weak,' says Martha and when she turns her back Eugenie pours the blackest of brews and lightens it only a little with milk. Chelsea takes it with a grin, not sure she should be so happy.

'So,' says Sarah, who has long silver plaits neatly intertwined with blue ribbons that match her eyes, 'little thief.'

'Little thief,' Virginia repeats with a smile. Her hair is iron-grey, short and wavy, and her eyes an indeterminate mix of yellow and brown. 'You know, they used to accuse witches of stealing milk straight from the cows, leaving them with empty udders. Did you know?'

Chelsea is silent, but her gaze goes wide.

'Bottles are more convenient,' says Eugenie lightly. She's got more colour left in her hair than the others, black but with many rivers of white, coarser, thicker than the rest, like serpents with minds of their own.

Martha, ash-blonde, green-eyed, just butters more toast, adds lime marmalade without asking if the girl likes it. Chelsea, thievery notwithstanding, has good manners and eats it without complaint—plus, she's starving. Martha says, 'Little thief, tell us your tale before we pass judgment.'

'I ...' Chelsea looks around, takes note of the three cats sitting on the sill of the kitchen window, all watching her attentively as if what she says next is of great importance. She's old enough to understand that her position is one of shame; not because of the theft so much as being a child whose parents cannot feed them adequately. The shame isn't hers, but she still feels it, suffers for it on her mother's behalf. She says lamely, 'I leave home too early for breakfast.'

And the faces of the Widows are all painted in varied shades of disappointment. Not much surprise, and a lot of understanding. But still, disappointment. Silence hangs for a long moment.

'Hungry thief, then.' Sarah's gentle expression doesn't waver.

'Well, you need to make restitution,' says Eugenie sharply. 'We need help around the house, especially Martha in that damned garden.'

'I'd be happy of a scribe,' chimes Virginia. 'I'm cataloguing the library.'

'Sarah will be bottling jams and preserves soon enough,' says Eugenie.

'What do *you* need me for?' ventures Chelsea.

'I've no need of help.' Eugenie looks the girl up and down as if finding her of no use. It's not a mean glance, just frank.

'Then it's settled,' Martha announces, and no one gainsays her. 'Your penance will be to come here for breakfast before school every week day. And after school, there will be chores.'

'For how long?' asks Chelsea.

'Until your debt is worked off or you're no longer hungry.'

The girl nods slowly, then looks at them in turn, as if reluctant to bring up a problem. 'My mother ...'

'Never fear, my dear, we'll talk to your mother'—Virginia raises a finger to forestall any objections—'but we'll not mention the small matter of dairy larceny.'

'Thank you!' Chelsea smiles with relief. 'My mother worries, she gets stressed ...'

All the Widows hide their lips of string, hearts warmed that the girl is kind enough to defend her parent, but hardened that the child must lie to keep herself protected from the truth.

She looks apologetic now as she adds, 'I do need to get to school. If I'm late ...'

'Here.' Martha hands her a paper bag. 'A sandwich and

some fruit. Don't throw anything away, Chelsea Margaret Bloom.'

Virginia sees her to the door.

It's only when she gets down the stairs, retrieves her bike from the maw of the gate, that Chelsea realises between her capture and her breakfast she hadn't ever given the Widows her name.

'The mother works at Abi Hobbes' place sometimes,' Virginia says as all four of them cluster at the largest window in the parlour (where the Widows have been known to read fortunes for the townsfolk and whisper charms for the lovelorn), and watch Chelsea pedal off down the street towards Mercy's Brook High. Thin legs pump up and down, and flossy blonde hair flies behind her like something woven of spider webs. The heel of one sneaker is flapping, her jeans have been washed fragile, and her red t-shirt's faded beneath a coat that's nowhere near warm enough.

'Pretty woman, terrible waitress,' adds Eugenie. 'Always gets the order wrong.'

'Always?' Martha asks.

'Always. It's a talent, if you think about it,' Eugenie says with a shrug. 'Consistency is rare.'

'That's surprisingly generous of you.'

Sarah interrupts to cut off the inevitable bickering. 'That girl needs new clothes for a start. The problem at home?'

'The mother's boyfriend,' says Virginia.

The Widows have been observing Chelsea Margaret Bloom for the better part of a week. Alerted by the cats, they'd watched her from the upper windows the first day she stole a bottle of milk, and every day thereafter. They took in her expression, her general demeanour, the fact she looked half-starved and all scared. They started making enquiries around Mercy's Brook. At Abi Hobbes', Eugenie and Sarah began a discussion about daughters with other women who were there. Everyone chimed in but Ellie Bloom, who showed a striking lack of interest in joining the conversation, which the Widows noted. And they also noted, when Sarah introduced the topic of husbands, boyfriends and lovers, that Ellie was only too anxious to chat about her beau, Teddy Landreneau.

Teddy was a mechanic, employed at Hannigan's Garage; a man with long black hair, dark eyes, and pock-marked skin. He was not Mercy's born, nor was he pretty but he was big, seemed like he might be protective—which was a mistake several women before Ellie Bloom had made. Others might continue to make it too, if she ever got her head right and gave him the boot. At the moment, however, that seemed unlikely. They'd been seeing each other for four months, living together for two (which was convenient, whispered Abi Hobbes, after he'd been thrown out of his own apartment for fighting and not paying his rent—Sheriff Taylor had had to deliver warnings to him on more than one occasion). And these last two months, rumour had it, coincided with Chelsea Margaret Bloom looking thinner than she was genetically wont to be and terrified to boot. The Widows had seen plenty of girls with that same look, and they recognised it the first day she'd stolen their milk.

Now, while Sarah buttered more toast, Martha poured more coffee and asked, 'Who should take Mr. Landreneau?'

'Me. I love a bully,' says Eugenie.

'Play to one's strengths. I'll try talking to Ellie Bloom, then,' says Martha.

'Good luck,' says Virginia with an uncharacteristic sneer.

'Now, now. There's always hope,' Sarah says gently. 'In one form or another.'

'You know where I'll be then,' Virginia finishes; she goes

to one of the cupboards and pulls out a bright blue vial. 'I'll have this ready soon.'

School had never been enjoyable, but Chelsea kept her head down and didn't draw attention; she didn't yearn for friends or a greater connection, she did her homework assiduously, made sure her marks were good enough to keep her below anyone's concern radar. She loved reading and spent her lunch hours and free periods in the library. Chelsea tried to make herself as small as she could, so no one noticed her and she didn't attract her mother's random tempers; she was doing well at it until Teddy entered Ellie's life and, by unfortunate association, hers as well.

Yet it had been manageable until he moved in with them.

That crossing over, that incursion, caused a bleed in the rest of her life. She became actively miserable and *that* drew notice to her as surely as a beacon. The mean girls, like tall blonde Becky Silverman, suddenly found in her a target for their barbs. Worse, the bully boys whose eyes had passed over her unseeing for so long, suddenly saw her. Her schoolwork suffered, which meant teachers who'd had no concern for her now talked about her in the staff room as a 'worry'. It didn't occur to Chelsea that her previous invisibility had been a kind of magic, something she could do without thinking, but also something that could, unfortunately, be easily sent awry by unhappiness because, unaware of it, she wasn't in conscious control of it.

Since the shift in Chelsea's universe, since the veils around her parted, she's been in Becky Silverman's sights, which would have been bad enough on its own. But unfortunately Becky's best boyfriend also noticed Chelsea; it wasn't like he was paying her court or anything nice. But Becky's kind of fucked-up about relationships, and can't tell the difference between what's healthy and what's not, so even though Evan's been making jokes at Chelsea's expense, it's enough to set Becky's jealousy off like a rocket.

So, this afternoon, during English, which is the last class of the day, when Chelsea asks to go to the bathroom, Becky follows. Chelsea can hear the footsteps behind her in the hall, risks a glance over her shoulder and clocks the look on the other girl's pretty face. It's enough to make her break into a run. She knows Becky's faster than her, too, coz she's on the track and field team, but that's no reason not to try to escape.

As Chelsea bangs through the big double doors into the fresh air she trips on the flapping sole of her sneaker. She tumbles down the stairs, grazing elbows, the knees of her jeans tear away to leave the skin of her legs vulnerable to bruises and cuts. As she rolls to a stop, she finds a pair of old suede boots, red in colour, very close to her nose. Chelsea cranes her neck to see a pair of black leggings, a burgundy tunic and a thick knitted long black cardigan. Yellow-brown eyes, iron-grey hair, and a kind smile look down at her.

'Trouble brewing?' Virginia asks, just as Becky Silverman skids out.

'Bitch,' spits Becky from the top of the stairs. Her features twist, blonde curls do too, like snakes. Whatever has drawn this spite out of her, it's Medusa-like in nature. She begins to curse up a blue storm that might even put a blush in Eugenie's cheek.

'Now, now, girl. If you can't say anything nice, don't say anything at all.' Virginia's right hand barely moves, but the fingers curl upward elegantly, and abruptly the stream of profanities coming from Becky's mouth ceases. Not by her will, though, for she keeps trying, and her eyes grow wider with every passing second that she fails to produce a sound. Virginia smiles, and the malign expression looks a little ill-fit on that gentle face.

She reaches a hand down to Chelsea, who takes it with only a tiny hesitation.

'How long ... ?' asks the girl as she hurries down the path beside the old woman, whose pace is more leisurely.

'Long enough to teach her a lesson.' Virginia smiles again, and it's less frightening. 'Come along, we need to get you some new clothes.'

'My mother ...'

'Oh, darling. We both know your mother won't be looking for you.' Then to soften the blow, she adds, 'Don't worry, Martha is making arrangements.'

Eugenie spends her morning sitting in a café across from Hannigan's Garage, making bad coffee and a stale pastry last. The roller doors are up, so she can see Harper Hannigan and his employees moving back and forth as they work. Eugenie makes a mental note to talk to Harper about his choice in workers; Sookie Delorme is fine, been with him for thirteen years, but Teddy Landereau was clearly a mistake.

He's muscular, for sure, and Eugenie lets her mind wander a little, but when lunchtime comes and Teddy heads off towards the low-rent diner a ways down the street he goes to everyday, she's all business. She leaves money on the table, a generous tip, and a lot of crumbs, then follows Teddy with a stride not her own: it's a hobble, really, an old lady's gait. It distracts people; no one notices harmless little old ladies with limps.

But before he reaches the diner, Teddy takes a detour, nips between the iron gates in the fence around the rambling park. Eugenie puts on a burst of speed now, no sign of the slowness of age or infirmity; she buries her hands in her coat pockets, clenching the fists to loosen the aching fingers, the right one fidgeting with the item she finds there. The trees are thick at the entrance, so she hurries to get the mechanic in sight again, sees his broad back at last, disappearing around another bend.

If she'd given it any thought, which she doesn't because she's concentrating on pursuit, she might realise he's gotten farther away than he should, even on his long legs; that he's run while he's been out of her sight. That he's drawing her deeper into the park, farther from the main thoroughfare, farther from the ears and eyes of witnesses, farther from potential aid.

Eugenie's sturdy boots make no sound on the path and that's probably what saves her: Teddy's not quite ready when she rounds the corner, so he's slow in swinging the thick branch, which in turn gives her a little time in which to jump backwards.

He catches her a glancing blow, however, and she's knocked off balance. She totters, is amazed that he caught her where her late unlamented husband Sidney always used to. The pain in her left breast is astonishing, and she remains incredulous that she never developed cancer there, after all the abuse; but it's over her heart, and she knows that's where all the true damage was done.

Still and all, she's grateful: if Teddy'd been prepared he'd probably have taken her head off, or at least given it a damned good rattling. And to her advantage, his mis-swing upset his equilibrium, and so gains her a few seconds. She pulls her hands out of her pockets (*Honestly, Eugenie! Hands in pockets, how can you defend yourself that way?*), the right one tugs the wooden thing up ... and the thing makes a hollow wooden *pokpokpok* as it hits the ground, fumbled by her stiff fingers.

Eugenie scrambles after it, but finds herself hauled back and held aloft. She's surprised though she knows she shouldn't be, at his automatic unprovoked violence against an old woman. What could possibly cause this? Being followed by an ostensibly harmless relict?

Now she's being dangled. Her toes barely touch the dirt, the tips of her boots making a soft scrap. She feels like a cat held by its scruff.

'Bitch!' Teddy sneers, breath reeking of cigarettes and old meat hits Eugenie in the face. 'What the fuck do you want?'

She manages in her best cowardly quaver, 'Why are you hurting me? I was just taking a walk!'

'Bullshit! You've been watching me all morning.'

'I was going to feed the pigeons!' She injects, she hopes, just the right note of innocent despair. She always carries seed in her coat pockets in case she needs a cover; prefers to feed the ravens, but pigeons are more numerous, less note-worthy, more mundane.

He glares at her with eyes so dark that pupil and iris are indistinguishable; whatever he sees in her face seems to convince him. Teddy throws her away.

She lands awkwardly, and feels the little finger of her right hand twist entirely the wrong way. Eugenie lets the cry out even though her natural instinct is to bite down on it. But it will make her seem *innocuous*. She scoops up what looks like a twig covered in thorns, and feels it puncturing her fingers; it doesn't matter, she's immune after all this time. And her grip's tight, determined.

Eugenie stands, shuffles over to Teddy Landreneau, who's now regarding her with utter disinterest. She moves past him as if to continue on her way. He doesn't even turn his head to watch her passage, so dismissive is he, and that's when she takes the opportunity to slash the twig down the back of his left hand. It's fast-acting, the poison, digitalis-based, some paralytic in there too so he doesn't even have the moment required to make a fist. Then he's tilting and tipping surely as a felled tree, landing with much the same shuddering effect on the earth. It'll look like a heart attack; the scratches look quite natural, something he'd incur in the fall.

The Widows are clever and careful.

Eugenie stands tall, looks at her handiwork; the only effect the poison has on her is a slight numbing in her hand, which she welcomes as it means she can't quite feel the pain in her fractured little finger. It'll do until she gets home and Martha can attend to the injury properly.

Virginia has walked Chelsea home, neither saying much, and now they're at the mouth of the dank little street where the girl shares a dank little house with her mother. Virginia stops very firmly beneath the sign that reads "Erebus Drive"; she won't go further. She turns Chelsea to face her so the girl cannot see the police cruiser parked in the driveway of Number 42, then hands over three shopping bags.

'Make sure your mother knows these were a gift.'

Chelsea nods. 'Thank you, Miss Virginia. I don't—'

Virginia holds up her hand. 'Chelsea, your mother's going to be a bit upset. I'm given to understand that something's happened to Teddy.' Virginia pretends not to see the look of hope on the girl's face. She pulls a bright blue bottle from her pocket; it's stoppered with a small cork and sealed by red wax. It has no label.

'How do you—'

'Hush. You'll learn that good and bad news travel at the same speed, but via different messengers.' Virginia drops the bottle into one of the shopping bags. 'This will help her sleep tonight, and tomorrow she'll be a new woman. Five drops, that's all, then bring the bottle back to us when you're done.'

Virginia touches Chelsea's cheek. 'Remember that you are welcome with us anytime. Should you need a refuge, our home is yours. The same goes for your mother. She is also welcome.'

'Thank you, Miss Virginia.' Chelsea smiles, then her face clouds over. 'What about—'

'Oh, Becky will be back to normal tomorrow morning and more's the pity. But you'll find her less willing to trouble you, I'll be bound. And, Chelsea?'

The girl says nothing, just waits with bated breath.

'We will teach you how to deal with ones such as her, how to walk in the shadows for your own safety. You need only attract attention when you wish.'

And Chelsea thinks this is the most wonderful news she's ever heard, even better than Teddy's accident. She gives Virginia a swift, hard hug that drives the air out of the lungs of the older woman, who laughs and hugs back.

Chelsea turns down the street towards her home, which looks even bleaker than it ever has; she stumbles a little, seeing the sheriff's car parked outside, then recovers, mindful of Virginia's comment about Teddy. She throws a glance over her shoulder, gives the Widow a wave, and moves on to disappear up the broken path to number 42 Erebus Drive.

Ellie Bloom's been crying for about two hours now. It didn't take long for Teddy Landreneau's body to be discovered by joggers, and it took even less time for Sheriff Taylor to call by and let Ellie know that he was gone from her life. The bruises on Ellie's cheeks and wrists made Sheriff Janey Taylor wonder if it was any loss at all but that didn't seem to slow the tears. After a while, she began to wonder where Chelsea was, because surely it was time for the girl to be home from school? Not that she wanted to leave Chelsea alone to deal with her mother, but she couldn't quite figure out what she could do to fix the situation. Janey had had men like Teddy Landreneau in her life when she was young, her own mother had collected them like bad pennies, but when she lost her calm and said, 'C'mon, Ellie. You know you're better off without him, don't you?' Ellie just howled louder.

Sheriff Taylor is therefore quite relieved to hear the jingle of keys in the front door, and the sound of light footsteps along the short hallway. Janey hurries to meet her before she steps into the sitting room.

'Chelsea!'

'Hello, Sheriff.'

'Chelsea, some bad news, I guess. Teddy …'

But Chelsea just nods, and Janey realises the girl already knows. The Sheriff didn't think to ask how: Mercy's Brook was small enough that news flew like a winged thing. 'You give me a call if you need anything. I'll drop by tomorrow to check on you, promise.'

'Okay, thanks.' And Chelsea sees Janey out, takes a deep breath, then goes into the sitting room where her mother weeps on the loveseat.

'Teddy's gone!' Ellie manages through snot and tears.

'I know, Momma. I heard.'

'And you don't even sound a bit sorry!' Ellie's tone is sharp as a knife, but Chelsea doesn't deny the accusation.

'Momma, he wasn't good for you.'

'He looked after me! Loved me! Treated you like a daughter!'

And that last comment takes Chelsea's breath away. If Teddy's behaviour was paternal, then no wonder the world was so fucked up. Before she can form a response, Ellie starts in again.

'And now you want to leave me! My own daughter! Ungrateful!'

'No, Momma, no! Why would you think that?' But Chelsea's voice trembles, knowing it's true.

'That woman came here! That old bitch! Said they want to

teach you. They'll take you, take you away like they did those other girls! Taken from their own good mothers ...'

Chelsea thinks about the girls fostered by the Widows, how they finished high school, then went on to college. Sometimes they come back to visit. When they do, Mercy's Brook stops to watch, all the gossips churning internally, whispering and sniping. Some stayed here, made lives, but all their mothers went off on travels when their daughters moved into Widows' Walk and have never returned from their holidays and have not been seen since as she can recall.

Ellie might not feel quite so attached to her offspring had she not lost Teddy so recently; nor if Martha's visit this morning wasn't so fresh in her mind. All she can think of is the older woman's voice, quite reasonable at first as she proposed Chelsea spend some time being tutored by the Widows. Then, she finally lost her temper and said, 'You know, Ellie Bloom, you're meant to care more about what comes out of your cunt than what goes into it. I'm not quite sure if you'll ever learn that lesson, but I do hope you get the chance at some point.'

'I'll get you a drink, Momma, to calm your nerves, then we can talk about all this.'

In the tiny yellow kitchen Ellie finds a clean red wine glass and fills it to the brim with white wine from a box in the refrigerator. She's put the three shopping bags on the kitchen table, grateful that Ellie had been too distracted by her grief to ask where they'd come from. She digs the blue vial out of one of the bags, tips five drops in, resisting the urge to tip in more (an act of restraint of which the Widows would approve), then stirs it in with her finger. She needn't have bothered, the fluid is clear as water.

She hands it to her mother, curled on the loveseat by the window, the crocheted blanket wound around her lap. Chelsea goes to sit on a chair opposite. She doesn't say anything, but watches as Ellie guzzles the liquid down with barely a pause.

'Now, Momma ...'

'Oh, my, that is strong.'

And as Chelsea watches, something strange happens: Ellie's outline begins to change, to soften, her weeping changes to something new, something sharper and higher, a feline plaint.

The wine glass falls to the carpet with a soft thud. Where Ellie Bloom once sat there's a pretty tortoiseshell cat, with long whiskers and a floofy tail, green eyes, and an expression of surprised displeasure.

Chelsea finds a cat carrier in the garage, dusty, with a sprinkling of mice droppings across the top, from back when they'd had a pet. Chelsea packs her few treasures into the shopping bags. There isn't much she wants to keep.

She locks the door behind her and leaves the house on Erebus Drive, makes the shortish walk to Carter Lane. Ellie meows loudly the whole way there; she's heavy too, not just sitting in one spot but prowling the bottom of the cage as much as she can. Chelsea pauses at the fence, staring up at the big house. The closed gate clicks open without her having to touch it, and there's only the smallest hesitation before she steps through.

Tomorrow, Sheriff Taylor will drop over for morning tea and the Widows will let her know that Ellie Bloom's gone for a little holiday, that Chelsea will be staying with them for a while. Sheriff Taylor will look at the pretty new tortoiseshell cat sitting on the window ledge beside the black cat and give both a nod. Janey Taylor knows every inch of this house, having been fostered here herself. She will recall the Widows telling her that the transformation only lasts as long as the mothers remain selfish; the black cat's never changed back into her own mother. She will wonder if Ellie Bloom will one day walk on two legs again. She will smile and pat Chelsea Margaret Bloom on the shoulder before she advises the girl to be careful with her shoes—the cats often register their disapproval in unpleasant ways, at least until they get used to their new living arrangements.

THE WRONG GIRL

'The problem is,' she says as she spears a piece of crispy bacon skilfully enough that it doesn't shatter, 'you've got a revolving door for a heart.'

He doesn't like hearing things like this, mostly because she's generally right. Ilsa's clear-eyed about him. and that makes their friendship remarkably unfraught (apart from *these* moments). Unlike his other relationships. She *sees* him for who he is, but doesn't stop talking to him, doesn't judge him, not really, or if she does, she's still friends with him. His father used to say he was his own worst enemy, and he wonders if that's what she thinks. They talk about other things, laugh, it's not always about his failings or her intolerance; it couldn't be, or they'd never last five minutes, let alone five years. Maybe the friendship runs on pity. He'll take that.

She's pretty, beautiful even, but she doesn't look the way he needs her to, the way that sends him into a romantic frenzy. And she's got no interest in him, which he finds fascinating. Resents a little too; it's strange to have someone so ... *unmoved* by you. Almost insulting. And relieving, he supposes.

You're a very bad bet, she's said before, *and I've done my time with narcissists.*

Why do you keep talking to me? he'd asked.

You're decorative. You're smart. You're funny. And I don't have to date you.

'That's not fair.' He broke up with Clementine two days ago, some sympathy might be in order. He pushes the café's all-day-breakfast scrambled eggs around his plate. He's already swallowed the blue corn tacos down: they'd ordered at the same time, but when he'd seen her meal, his eyes went wide and he'd ordered again as a second course. She'd observed more than once that was the truth of him, his only true love was food, and he should thank the gods for his freakish metabolism. 'I just ...'

'You *just* put them on a pedestal from the start, you turn them into goddesses and even goddesses are imperfect, so there's nowhere for them to go but down in your estimation. You romance them, you make them think they're *the* one, that you're exactly who they've been looking for; you mimic what they want, then you get bored. Sooner or later, you start to drift. And you know what? You've showered them with such attention, such radiance, then you take away the sun.' She waves a fork at him, the scrambled egg on the tines sways hypnotically. 'And these are not stable women. I know that's your type. I know why, but for fuck's sake: you *know* you do this. You have to start taking responsibility.' She waves the fork again and he can't take his eyes off the eggs, yellow and white swirled. 'You have to stop dating avatars of your mother.'

'Hey, that's *really* not fair!' He reaches for the mug of long black, but his hands don't make it. Instead they curl up into fists he doesn't know what to do with.

You keep dating versions of my sister, she thinks, but refrains from saying because it's best he never meets Sophia or even knows she exists. It's amazing the range of things you can avoid talking about with friends; the stuff you choose to not offer up. Besides, she lives two states away and doesn't bother with Ilsa most of the time because there's always a boyfriend around to take up Soph's attention. Her sister occasionally calls, doesn't leave messages if Ilsa doesn't pick up—and Ilsa hasn't picked up in forever—there's just that long list of *missed call* notifications, like the one last week.

Ilsa stares at Will a moment longer. *His face writes cheques that his nature can't cash*, she thinks, watching as he blushes, eyes flicker down, those thick lashes seeming to take a bow. Such a pretty face. 'Why do you do it, then?'

'I just ...' Lunch isn't going the way he'd planned. Clementine had been a trial, she'd cut up his favourite hoodie, put his best Nikes into the InSinkErator. They'd only been together two months, so surely that was an overreaction? Surely he deserved a kind word? Surely?

Ilsa's tired, she's been working a lot of late nights because the exhibition's coming up and she's still got several pieces to finish. So, she's got less patience than normal for Will and his standard bullshit; what she'd usually find amusing is, today, just fucking vexatious, and she doesn't have the resources to keep that under control.

'Look, you'll never put what's right above your idea of *true love*.' She makes air quotes, and he feels like he's been flicked with acid. 'And true love doesn't fucking exist, at least not your concept of it. You're like a dog chasing a car: if you ever catch it, the bumper will knock your pretty face in. One day you'll pick the wrong girl.' She drops her fork, grabs her handbag and pushes back from the table. 'Wake up to yourself.'

He watches her walk out. It's not as if she's storming either, there's not even enough emotion in her for a rage. It's just her usual long-legged, earth-eating stride. He's no more than an irritation, and that cuts.

. . .

Ilsa spends the rest of the afternoon running errands, sourcing new brushes and paints, some groceries because she's let the pantry run down the past few weeks and even the pasta has been reduced to three pieces of penne and some lengths of spaghetti and there's not even a tin of tomatoes to drown them in. When the Uber lets her off outside her townhouse, she frowns.

There's a light in the front bedroom of the top floor. She can't recall turning it on.

When she gets through the gate and onto the little porch, she finds the door's unlocked. Ilsa puts the bags of food and art supplies down quietly, then slips the slim tactical baton from her tote; a souvenir of a policeman ex-boyfriend who wondered for a while where it went. She flicks it to full-length —*snik*—then steps inside.

The house is narrow, three-storeys, renovated last year when her paintings started selling for stupid money. She could have moved but she likes it here, besides, the attic studio is exactly how she wants it. From the hallway she can see all the way down to where the kitchen and dining room wait, a lambent glow from the lights she *definitely* didn't leave on. There's the rattle and clack, the soft thud of someone going through drawers and cupboards, the hushed protest of the fridge closing without the aid of a push: the strange sideways gravity of expensive appliances.

Ilsa holds the baton high as she steps around the doorframe into the kitchen. She can feel her lips peeling back from her teeth, a familiar rictus of rage and affront: how dare anyone invade her space? She's bringing the billy-club down as she swings in, sees her sister's pale face, eyes wide, mouth an 'o' as she drops a plate on the tiled floor, watching the weapon descend like an axe.

. . .

'Your face!' Sophia says, clutching at her chest dramatically. 'I thought you were going to kill me.'

'Don't be silly. I didn't know it was you.' Ilsa sips a glass of the white wine Sophia brought with her. 'Besides, you don't want a home invader to think you're fucking around.'

They're in the sitting room. The shards of the broken plate have been cleared away, Ilsa's laid out a platter of cheese and crackers; Sophia's meal-related forward planning only ever encompasses booze. Behind the glass, the flames of the gas-fire are leaping against the chill of an autumn evening.

'How'd you get in, Sophia?' asks Ilsa.

'Now, you only call me that when I'm in trouble.'

'Not in trouble, no. Soph.' Sophie and Soph when she was good; Sophia when she wasn't.

'The spare key's under the porch rail. Just like it was at home.' Sophia smiles, smug. *See? I'm clever too.*

Not quite, thinks Ilsa: at "home", it was stuck on the underside with a lump of Blu-Tack from God-knows-where that retained its stickiness well beyond the natural lifespan of such things. Here, in her neat townhouse, her place, her sanctuary, the key's in a small metal box, a magnet keeps it attached to the steel plate the builder screwed beneath the rail. She'd decided against a coded lockbox, but maybe she should think about it again. If *this*—her sister—was going to become a habit.

Ilsa sighs, reaches for a cracker, a sliver of brie. 'Soph, if you'd let me know you were coming—left an actual message— I'd have made arrangements. I wouldn't have been so surprised. Anyway, what's wrong, you can't talk to a machine?'

'I came on a whim, Ilsa, you know how I am. Besides, I hate leaving voicemails.'

'What's ...' Ilsa trawls her memory for the name of the last one, 'Digby think of that?'

'Rigby. We're on a break.' Sophie's glance slips away, finds the flames.

Broke up, thinks Ilsa. 'What about work?'

'They owe me a lot of leave.'

Fired, thinks Ilsa.

'So, I thought I'd come and visit my big sister.'

Freeload, thinks Ilsa.

Ilsa sighs again, but only internally. A second visual sign of exasperation will bring on one of Sophia's traditional tantrums, and Ilsa's already exhausted from brunch with Will. So she smiles instead and sips her wine, praying it might give her some sort of strength, more than she's currently got for dealing with difficult people.

'The spare room's liveable,' she says, and it's more than that because she's always prepared. 'I'll put fresh sheets on the bed while you take a shower—or a bubble bath, there's a huge tub.'

'Thank you, sissy,' says Sophia, and smiles, and Ilsa sees the little girl she used to be, so small when their mother brought her home from the hospital. *Ilsa's doll*, Momma said, when what she meant was that Ilsa would be looking after the baby because Momma had other things to do.

Ilsa thinks how much she'd loved her sister before Sophie discovered boys and decided she needed attention in order to live; that as long as she could see herself reflected in the twin mirrors of some guy's gaze, then she had worth, she had value, she *existed*. She'd got that from their mother, along with the long blonde hair and soulful brown eyes that looked hurt even when they weren't.

It had taken years but yes, Ilsa's sisterly love had dimmed, and a kind of pitying contempt took its place. You can only hurt for so long, Ilsa knows. The fact she couldn't rely on her sister—support only went one way—meant that Ilsa had gradually let contact between them die. She'd known, somehow, that if she didn't make the effort, then nothing would happen (except missed phone calls that'd only mean requests and demands if you'd answered), but letting something like that occur (that *dying*) takes time—you have to be able to *allow* it. It confirms all your worst fears, she thinks, that you've loved too foolishly for too many years. Even blood ties can't make up for that.

Their parents were long gone, there were no children, nephews or nieces, that might have made an effort seem worthwhile. The threads between them had become thin as spider webs, things that could only be noticed if you looked carefully, only obvious on rainy days when droplets made the silken lines visible. But now, seeing Sophie, Ilsa ached. Ached for the old closeness, for what they'd once had. She ached to feel, just for a moment, that her sister was *hers* and always would be. Even if it was a lie, and Ilsa wasn't given to believing such things.

The ache, though, it plied a little crack in her heart and she scolded herself. *It will end as it always does, with the butterfly departing on a whim, taking my favourite jeans and earrings, and leaving roughly the same devastation in its wake as a tornado.* Following some man who has eyes like mirrors, eyes that made promises they couldn't or wouldn't keep.

But still: the breach has been made, and even *her* heart's susceptible to hope and the inevitable future fracturing.

It's two days later, when she's up in the studio, that the doorbell rings. Ilsa doesn't think anything of it, because there are always deliveries of books and supplies, occasionally flowers from a suitor, although those have been few and far between for a couple of months. That's okay, she's got more than enough to occupy her time, and when she desires attention again, it won't be a problem. It's a want, not a need, and she recognises it as such. Ilsa's never *needed* to see herself in someone else's gaze.

The advantage of having her sister around is that Sophie can sign for parcels without Ilsa having to stop what she's doing. After a couple of hours, she pauses and heads downstairs for some lunch. She's careful to lock the door because Sophia's curious as a cat and has no sense of boundaries, and the last thing Ilsa needs is her sister wittering on in the studio while she's trying to work.

There are voices coming from the sitting room. Ilsa frowns: surely not even Soph would invite the delivery guy in for a drink? She thinks again, seems to recall that Digby-Rigby worked for FedEx when Soph moved him into her place a few years ago. But no, it's worse. The tones get clearer as she gets closer. Her heart spasms with realisation. Bile bubbles and she tells herself it's stupid, an overreaction. She's being melodramatic, behaving like Sophia at her best or worst. Ilsa tells herself that.

On her expensive leather sofa, sitting too close, are Sophia and Will, smiling at each other as if those are the only expressions they ever wear, as if those smiles will never stop, as if those smiles are only ever for each other. As if they've been waiting for this very moment, this very meeting. They don't look up when Ilsa enters the room. They don't look up when she leaves without a word, the pit of her dropping away into an unplumbed abyss.

It lasts six whole weeks, and it's unbearable.

Sophia, when she's home, sits on the edge of Ilsa's bed at all hours of the night, singing Will's perfections and asking why Ilsa had never introduced them. Ilsa doesn't bother explaining, old experience has taught her that Sophia doesn't listen to anything that doesn't support what she wants. *I just never thought of it and besides, you live so far away*, she says, and hopes it will pass quickly. That Will gets bored sooner rather than later, that Sophia finds a new reflective surface somewhere else, that she swiftly returns home, is out of Ilsa's hair and life.

She hopes her sister will soon be gone.

Will's not much in evidence at the townhouse, he knows better than to push his luck. He just drives by, collects Sophia, takes her away, sometimes for days at a time. But she's always returned in the end, like it's a custody arrangement Ilsa never agreed to.

It lasts six long weeks.

Then Will's heart, inevitably, begins to change.

He's seen all Sophia's facets and moods and some of them aren't pretty. No prettier than his, frankly—and in the end, he doesn't really want to be with someone who reminds him of himself. Her gaze, at first so compelling, flattering, was a focus of attention that made him the centre of the universe. But eventually it began to feel like she wasn't adding to him, but taking away ... draining him.

It wasn't quite the same as usual, less a boredom and more a kind of fear, but it had the same result, in the end.

I think we should spend some time apart.

I think we should see other people, so we appreciate each other more.

I've started to think of you as a friend, and I don't want to hurt you ...

Even though it was well past the time when hurt might not be done.

He *had* liked her, a lot.

He'd gone to the townhouse to continue the argument with Ilsa—he was sufficiently irritated two days after the fight—but he'd met Sophia, hadn't he? Initially, it was simply a means to get at Ilsa, but he hadn't intended to begin something only to end it. *Of course, he never intended to break up*—he could almost hear Ilsa's voice in his head—but it always happened. He'd wanted to show Ilsa that he could do what she said he couldn't. And wasn't her sister the best way to do that? The best way to show her, to make her sister happy, to make Sophia his?

But Ilsa was right, and what always happened, happened yet again.

He thought Sophia had taken it well. She'd smiled, eyes a little glassy with unshed tears. He thought she was brave. She'd be fine.

It lasts six short weeks.

Ilsa finds Sophia in the bathtub, cold and unmoving. No note, nothing so dramatic, which is very much out of character for her sister. Maybe this last act was statement enough; in death, she'd finally learnt the art of understatement. The scalpel Sophia'd used—taken from a packet of newly delivered equipment—lay on the plush white bathmat, like a silver stem for the red blossoms that had dripped from one wrist.

Ilsa stares at her bloodless butterfly of a sister, and all she feels is cold. As if all her blood had flowed away with Sophie's. But there's no pain, no ache, no scream pushing its way out. She imagines they'll come later. When they're good and ready.

It's the day before the exhibition. Ilsa makes arrangements for the funeral, while her assistant takes care of the last details of the opening night; she'll bury Sophia the day after. No one knows her sister here—there was no chance to introduce her to any friends before she'd attached herself to Will. Ilsa doesn't tell anyone.

She doesn't tell Will, not even when he arrives at the exhibition.

She sees him standing by one of the pieces, one of the great red canvasses she's painted in a variety of materials, all studies in death and decay and rebirth. The theme is 'desire.' They're confronting and dramatic, bodies in motion and torment, long limbed and reaching. They've found favour with the rich who don't understand them, but covet all the same.

Will has some of her early work, before her prices got out of his league. Someone once offered him a lot for one of them, but he'd refused to sell. It's something he has of hers, and that's important.

At the opening, he thinks he's never seen Ilsa look so lovely. She's tall and slender, her hair is straight and dark, and there's an air to her that he recognises but can't understand for a moment. Then he realises: she's broken. He feels it more than he sees it, but it's there for sure. A fracture in her that wasn't there before. More than one, like she's a mirror that's been dropped, and fault lines run across her surface, though she's holding herself together.

She's irresistible, now.

She sees him and stares. He raises his glass and then, very slowly, she nods.

Ilsa circulates around the party; they circle each other unhurriedly, don't intersect until the end of the evening. It doesn't occur to Will that perhaps *this* is a bad idea. Only when most of the paintings have 'sold' stickers on, when the crowd has dispersed, and Ilsa has given her assistant final instructions, only then does Will approach. She says she wants to go back to her place. He hesitates. She says, 'Soph's not there anymore,' and he assumes they've had some sisterly falling out, that Sophia has gone back from whence she came. He doesn't ask any questions.

Ilsa still refuses to kiss him and it's driving him nuts. He should have realised she'd draw things out, he's known her long enough. She's not one for instant gratification.

There's another glass of wine and another, but he doesn't notice hers never empties, is never refilled. He's got other things on his mind. He's happy to follow her up to the attic studio when she suggests it. He's happy to let her tie him to the chair in the centre of the white-walled room lined with canvasses in various states of finishing. He thinks she'll straddle him, take him inside her, but she doesn't.

She stops answering questions, she begins making preparations, setting out buckets and bottles, lining up sharp silver objects along a bench. He starts to sober, just a little, just enough to take notice of the bigger jars on the metal shelving along one wall: a lot of red, thick and dark, with things floating in the liquid, too far away for him to distinguish what they are precisely, but enough to terrify him.

'Ilsa, I want to stop. I want to go home.' He hates that he sounds like a little boy.

'Didn't I tell you that one day you'd pick the wrong girl?' She shows him the photo on her phone, the one she took of Sophia in the crimson-filled tub, the one she took before she called emergency services even though it was well past an emergency.

Will looks at those bottles again, gazes around, notices at last the discarded mound of men's shoes in a corner. He thinks about all the boyfriends who've disappeared from her life, how they never troubled her again, no stalking, no insistence, damage contained. A rare woman untroubled by men who can't let go.

'You've such a pretty face. It would be a shame to waste it,' she says, and begins to cut.

A MATTER OF LIGHT

'Mr. Holmes,' drawled the butler with a haughty sniff, 'is not best pleased.'

Kit Caswell raised one fine eyebrow; she'd given her name so he could not have been ignorant of who she was. Besides, how many visitors might be expected this late at night in fashionable Piccadilly? And how many might have been received with this level of disdain? The written summons had come from John Watson, so technically it mattered not a jot what Mr. Holmes might or might not be displeased about, but she kept the thought to herself; for some reason servants seemed to like Holmes rather more than their betters did. She was unsure as to why, but thought perhaps it had something to do with the Great Detective's ability to make fools of said betters, all of which caused much amusement and satisfaction below stairs.

The good doctor's missive had been brief and finished with the admonition 'to dress like a lady'. Although the temptation to disobey had been strong Kit'd controlled herself. She wore a neat purple plaid stuff walking suit, a confection of a hat she couldn't really stand but upon which her housekeeper, Mrs. Kittredge, had insisted, a cloak against the chill evening air, and black kid gloves which she removed one carefully plucked finger at a time.

'Indeed?' she said and, leaning close enough to catch a whiff of a not-unpleasant odour, draped her cloak over the man's shoulder, enjoying his look of outrage. She slapped the slim gloves into the palm of the hand he raised in surprise; he had no choice but to grab at them, or let them drop thereby failing in his professional duty. Her reticule—containing house keys, handkerchief, several sovereigns, and a set of brass knuckles—she retained. 'Well, I have been summoned—I've not inflicted myself on this household uninvited—and thus I am arrived. Be so kind as to conduct me to Doctor Watson. We'd not want Mr. Holmes discontented any sooner than needs must.'

There were a few tense seconds when she thought he might instead shove her out into the night for sheer spite, but apparently his training was too ingrained. He choked, 'This way, Miss Caswell.'

A slight, pretty maid wearing a very clean white apron over a black dress—whatever had happened in this grand house meant that neither maid nor butler had a chance to change into their nightclothes though it was past midnight—appeared from a darkened doorway. She gathered the garments from the butler's hands, barely glancing at Kit beyond a measured flicker, yet it was enough to convey her opinion of the late-night visitor. Clearly it matched that of the butler.

Inwardly, Kit sighed and wished she'd stayed at home reading the book on Eastern European folklore. The light of her notoriety hadn't dimmed in the three months since she had, in no particular order, run to ground Jack the Ripper, become the fosterling of Sir William Gull, and been discovered masquerading as a man in the service of London's

Metropolitan Police Force, much to the consternation of her superiors. Everyone, from low born to high, seemed to think they had a God-given right to comment on her behaviour, either by verbiage or action. Mrs. Kittredge had a saying about opinions being like fundamental orifices: everyone had one and they produced much the same substance.

Kit grinned as she followed the butler's astonishingly straight back along a corridor filled with closed doors. Behind one she could hear in passing the sounds of muttering and pacing; from behind another came sobbing. An elegant house, noted Kit, big enough to accommodate an impressive entry hall, at least two drawing rooms, a library, a study, a formal dining room, and other reception rooms besides on its ground floor. There'd be a kitchen and laundry below, and bedrooms above, with servants quarters above that. Which made her wonder at the lack of other domestics—surely a legion would be required in a place like this? Shouldn't they be gathered in corners, whispering and milling?

When there was no further to go, the butler threw open the very last door with what might have been aplomb tinged with contempt: *There! I've done my duty but I take no pleasure in it!*

'Doctor Watson, Miss Caswell has arrived,' he announced darkly.

Kit stepped past him into a dimly lit room lined with books and redolent of hair oil, pipe smoke and paper. John Watson, on the shortish side, in his late thirties, moustache and hair touched by dignified though perhaps premature grey snow, sat at a desk that, had it been a person, could only have been described as 'dishevelled'. He looked up and smiled, hands filled with disparate folios and envelopes. She was fairly certain he'd not found what he was looking for, whatever that might have been. Parallel with the edge of the desk, a silk-lined box held a gleaming silver letter opener with a sharply honed edge, the placement of which suggested a missing twin, perhaps lost beneath the papers through which Watson was searching.

'Thank you, Peterson. That will be all. Oh, is Mr. Holmes still in the north parlour, and your mistress in the south?'

'Yes, sir. Shall I carry a message?'

Watson shook his head. 'Thank you, no.' He waited until Peterson had closed the door behind him and said in a low voice, 'It's always best to know where he is before one discusses him.'

Kit smiled. 'Are you well, sir?'

'Well, enough. My apologies for this late hour, but there is a matter which I believe will only respond to your particular talents, Miss Caswell.' He rose and came to offer his hand, which was square, his grip firm. His eyes brightened when he smiled.

'I'm happy to help you if I am able, Doctor Watson.'

'Well, helping me involves helping Holmes ...'

Kit pulled a face. The Great Detective had, like many others, made his opinion of her known, supplying quotes to any newsman who had asked. She was irresponsible, a girl playing at dress-ups, at best a hoyden, at worst some sort of jezebel or suffragette. Kit thinned her lips. She'd met Watson at a dinner party at Sir William's and found him kind and clever, surprisingly non-judgmental (some of her foster father's guests regarded her as a curiosity to be gazed upon much like Mr. Joseph Merrick or a bearded lady in a travelling show). The good doctor had made it clear he didn't share his friend's opinion in this matter at least, and they'd gotten along famously. She relented and said, 'Tell me what the problem is, Doctor, and I'll decide if I'm willing to assist.' She grinned. 'You mentioned my talents?'

'Let us call it your open-mindedness.'

'What has happened?'

He led her to a burnished walnut sofa covered with blue and gold brocade in front of the hearth where a fire burned low. 'Holmes has been … out of sorts of late. He does not do well when bored and you might recall my mention of his … tendencies.' In a moment of confidence, he'd let slip the man's recreational habits, how they had almost destroyed him and how he, Watson, had been at pains to keep his friend distracted. Easily solved cases provided some relief, but only temporarily like feeding an enormous hunger with tiny rare meals, or attempting to extinguish a raging fire with thimblefuls of water. Such small successes, such easy gains merely increased Holmes' thirst for challenge, made him more irritable and, Watson knew from old and painful experience, more susceptible to the siren song of his demons.

'And you believe this one to be one of those easily solvable, quickly digested puzzles that give him but brief satisfaction?' asked Kit.

'I fear now that it might be better if it had been.' Watson shook his head. 'I thought it might provide more fit meat for him to chew upon, but alas I fear it will only result in further frustration.'

'The details, Doctor?'

'Of course. Just the details.' He smiled. 'We are in the home of a Mr. and Mrs. Harrington. Mr. Harrington is a shipping magnate of some note, and considerable fortune. His wife is a society beauty, or rather was in her day,' he said, gaze softening, displaying signs of diverting from topic. 'Still, in a certain light—'

Kit tapped him on one wrist before he waxed lyrical about the lady's bygone loveliness. 'It's always a matter of light, Doctor, in all aspects of life and perspective.'

He raised a hand in surrender. 'Of course, irrelevancies. Here is our problem: Ezekiel Harrington is dead.'

'Thoroughly dead?'

'Very dead indeed, but rather improperly.'

'Aha. So you and Holmes were called in hope of discretion?'

Watson nodded. 'I have known Ezekiel for some time—we shared a club—and his wife sent for me. I brought Holmes along in the hope of staving off yet another crisis in his confidence.'

'And why have the police not yet been called in?'

'We have the weapon and the murderer, but ... he will not confess.' John Watson shook his head. 'And Holmes cannot seem to divine the means to make him do so.'

'Ah. And if Mr. Holmes cannot gain a confession, he cannot perform for the public and bask in their adoration.'

'That is harsh, Miss Caswell.'

'But true, dear man, do not deny it.' Kit had on occasion wondered if half of Holmes' prey simply caved in and confessed, beaten down by the impression the Detective gave that he knew all one's sins as if they'd been written down in a book.

'Not untrue, no.' He sighed. 'Yet there is something else, Miss Caswell, something I cannot quite put my finger on. Something is just not right about the young man we have in custody.'

'Apart from the fact you believe him to be a murderer?'

'Beyond that.' He shook his head. 'We could hand the lad over to the police and be done with it, but ...'

'Your intuition renders you uncomfortable.' She smiled gently. 'What makes you think I might gain disclosure where Sherlock Holmes cannot?'

Watson paused, pursed his lips. 'You've a gentle way with you, and besides, you've seen things that others have not. You are willing to accept something alternate—more things in Heaven and Earth and all that—where more rational minds will not consider any explanation that does not conform to particular parameters.'

Kit sat back, away from the dying flames that were suddenly too intense. Pearls of sweat broke out down the line of her spine. No doubt her benefactor, Sir William, had let slip matters that Kit had entrusted to him in confidence. She asked calmly, 'What makes you say that, Doctor? Who has spoken out of turn?'

Watson looked guilty, then revealed: 'I have been for some years an acquaintance of Inspector Makepeace.'

'Ah.' Kit offered a silent apology to Sir William. Edwin Makepeace, her former superior at the Met, had taken her under his wing and acted as a mentor. Though he'd figured she was a girl well before the secret was out, he'd still listened to and acted upon her theories. And it was he who'd carried her, bruised and bloodied, from the London sewers after she'd helped destroy Jack the Ripper, burning him in a witch-fire kindled by his victims—unfortunately not before that notorious killer had stabbed her. 'Talking out of school.'

'Don't judge him too harshly, he was ... perturbed by what he saw.'

He should have experienced it, thought Kit, not entirely bitterly. Her shoulder where the knife had entered still ached. 'So, you think my gentle touch and an open mind might hold the key to your mystery?'

'Perhaps.' He shrugged. 'Or perhaps you might simply lead Holmes in the right direction.'

'I strongly doubt Mr. Holmes will listen to one such as I, Doctor, but I'll do my best for you.' She smiled. 'Kindly introduce me to the Widow Harrington.'

'I'm terribly sorry for your loss, Mrs. Harrington,' said Kit, examining the woman who sat on a red velvet chaise longue—or rather it seemed she'd draped herself on the furniture like a cat, conscious of how she appeared even at this late hour. Indeed, conscious and careful of how the illumination from the lamps fell upon her; Kit couldn't help but wonder how much time the mistress of the house had spent examining the way light and shadow mingled, and which position would show her fading charms to their best advantage. Unlike the servants, she'd obviously been to bed at some point, and wore an elaborate house coat in midnight blue over a white nightgown; embroidered slippers covered her tiny feet. Golden curls tumbled artlessly over one shoulder. It was interesting, though not surprising, that even under a weight of grief the woman had taken time to make herself look pretty. Augusta Harrington was not a unique creature; her looks were her currency no matter how devalued.

'I don't understand why you're here, Miss Caswell. Why is she here, Doctor Watson?' Her voice was a fluttering thing, like a wounded butterfly. Large limpid green eyes blinked at Kit in confusion. The woman seemed barely awake, yet she must have been up for some time since news of her husband's demise had been brought to her.

'Miss Caswell is here to help, Mrs. Harrington. Please tell her your tale. Indulge us.'

A snort came from the gloomy corner in which the Great Detective had sequestered himself. His leather wingback chair groaned each time he shifted with restless energy. His hawk-like nose and high forehead were silhouetted against the light of the window. *How long would he sulk?* Kit pondered, but didn't bother to cast a glance in his direction.

'Please tell me how you found your husband.'

The woman gave a sob, then buried her face in a handkerchief. John Watson knelt beside her and grasped her free hand with chivalrous enthusiasm. Kit managed not to roll her eyes. The doctor's weakness for pretty faces—faded or not

—was well-known, but his admiration brought a response, which Kit doubted her most patient questioning ever would.

'Emily woke me,' she choked.

'The maid,' explained Watson.

'Emily said Ezekiel had been murdered. That ... the boy was responsible.'

'And what did you do?'

'Went to his bedchamber and found him ... found him ...'

'The room is as we found it,' said Watson. 'I'll show you when you wish.'

'Who is the boy?' asked Kit.

'Some wretch in whom Ezekiel had taken an interest,' sobbed the woman. 'How could he repay my dear husband so vilely?!'

'And what did you see?'

'My poor Ezekiel in bed, cold and dead.'

'What's his name? The boy.'

Mrs. Harrington appeared nonplussed at the change of direction. 'Milo.'

'Nothing else?'

'No. Not that I ever heard my husband say.' She sniffled, appeared to wonder why she'd never asked for it herself.

'Had your husband's habits changed since the boy joined the household?'

'That boy was never part of this house. I would not allow it. He would ... visit Ezekiel in the evenings.' The woman's tone was sharp.

'I see. Had your husband adjusted how he conducted his daily life, Mrs. Harrington? Changes in appetite and action, in ways small or large?'

Mrs. Harrington paused, as if considering new aspects of her marital state that had not occurred to her, then said, 'He slept in, went to the office much later. He was ... short-tempered on occasion. His appetite has not been what it was for some weeks.' She bit at her lips then opened her mouth as if the words caused her pain: 'And he wanted no company but Milo's.'

'And where was the boy in the bedroom? In relation to your husband's body?'

That question broke the woman and she began to sob. When the flood did not abate after several minutes, not even under John Watson's tender hushing and there-there'ing, Kit went to the door to call for one of the servants. She found the young maid already waiting anxiously, as if she'd been on the verge of charging to her mistress' rescue but had not quite yet found the courage.

'Emily,'—Kit assumed it was she—'please see to Mrs. Harrington.'

The bedroom was large, decorated in dark masculine tones; part of its area was utilized as a sitting room furnished with a two armchairs in front of the cold fireplace, a low table, a mahogany secretaire and a chocolate-coloured recamier set between a pair of high arched windows with thick brocade curtains drawn. Also accommodated were a canopied bed, a chest of drawers and an armoire. A mirror sat above the hearth, all gilt and glamour. The marble-topped washstand seemed somewhat redundant when a door sat ajar showing where a closet had been converted to a small bathroom.

The air was thick and redolent with the iron odour of a red death. Yet from the doorway where Kit stood, she could see the lumpen shape of a body beneath the covers on the right-hand side—her left—of the bed, but no sign of a struggle.

'Where's the boy?' asked Kit.

'Locked in the coal cellar.'

'Did he go quietly?'

'Very. He was somewhat stuporous.'

Kit scanned the room. 'And where are all the servants, Doctor?'

'Most have left to prepare the Harringtons' country house. The family were meant to go tomorrow morning.' The clock on the mantle struck one, and Watson corrected himself: '*This* morning.'

'When was Mr. Harrington found?'

'Mrs. Harrington was somewhat hazy on that, but the maid said about eleven-thirty.'

'Why did she check on him then, the maid? Was she called for?'

'She said she noticed the light burning under the door rather later than was the master's wont.'

'Aha.' Kit stepped into the room and approached the bed.

Ezekiel Harrington had been a dignified looking man in his early fifties and remained rather handsome even with the spatters of dried blood on his face. His neck had been cut, left to right, with the silver knife remaining in the wound, its hilt resting on the red-stained pillow beneath the man's head. Kit's eyes followed the path of the arterial spray, on the wall and the bedclothes.

'He did not fight back.'

'It would appear not,' came Holmes' voice from the corridor.

'Where was the boy when you first saw this?' Kit frowned.

Watson cleared his throat. 'Beside Ezekiel, on the bed, curled like a child against him.'

Kit made her way around to the other side, leaned over the coverlet and noted how the mattress appeared to have barely borne the weight of another body. 'But the boy was not *in* the bed, surely?'

'No,' said Watson in surprise. 'How can you tell?'

'Because there is a void on the linens where no blood has

landed—presumably where another body lay—and then there is blood on the edge of the coverlet. Not to mention that the rug beneath my shoes feels rather wet and squishy.' Kit straightened. 'Surely you noticed that, Mr. Holmes?'

The silence from the hallway spoke volumes.

'So, you think to test me rather than to share what knowledge you have gleaned, sir?' She sighed. 'Help me, Doctor, if you please; let us not derange the scene too much.'

Carefully, she and Watson pulled back the covers, folding them at the foot of the bed.

Ezekiel Harrington lay in his nightshirt, which was rucked up around his thighs, one of which was flecked with prick marks and blood.

'Good Lord,' said Watson.

'You've not seen this, Mr. Holmes?'

His voice was closer when he said, 'No.'

Holmes had moved into the room and was bending over the dead man. He pointed at the patches of dried blood, then said with certainty, 'False starts.'

'This is a new habit?' asked Kit, and Holmes nodded, meeting her eye for the first time.

'Related to the young man?' ventured Watson.

'Let us ask him. Would you mind fetching the mysterious Milo, Doctor?'

'But of course.'

'Take Peterson along, just in case.'

'He's a slip of lad, barely half of my weight dripping wet.'

'Nevertheless, humour me. Oh, and kindly send the maid Emily up first of all.'

When the good doctor had departed, Kit and Holmes stared at each other for a few moments.

'A respectable man's reputation might survive a private drug habit,' observed Kit. 'But not being caught with either a dead girl or a live boy.'

An unwilling snort of laughter came from the tall man's mouth.

'Where is his paraphernalia?' asked Holmes. 'There should be a syringe and one vial, at least, for the morphine.'

Kit restrained herself from saying *You would know* and instead said, 'I wonder about this'—and pointed to the sprays of blood—'Correct me if I'm wrong, for your experience will be greater than mine, but does not this pattern appear ... weaker than it might?'

'Opium and its derivatives will slow the heartbeat, the pulse, the strength at which blood is pumped out. I believe that's the effect we witness here.'

'So. We must locate the paraphernalia to support our thesis.'

'Yes.'

'Was this murder the result of a drug-induced rampage, Mr. Holmes?'

'Not if we're dealing with morphine: it is not something to excite the system, Miss Caswell.' He smiled ruefully. 'But then, I suspect you already know that and are humouring me.'

In his smile was a sweetness she'd not expected. Grudgingly, she decided the Great Detective couldn't be all bad if someone like John Watson gave his devotion to the man. Kit did not nod, but gave an answering grin. 'The good doctor said Mr. Harrington was a shipping magnate?'

'Yes.'

'Where do his ships sail?'

'All over, but with especial interests in the Baltic and the Balkans.'

A timid knock on the door interrupted anything further he might have said.

'Come in,' said Kit, noticing how the lanky man took up position by the curtained windows, finding refuge in shadow once more. Was that the truth of Sherlock Holmes? That he was only happy in the light when he was confident of his truth? Any uncertainty might risk the exposure of the ragged edges of him, the shattered nerves. No one but Watson was allowed that sort of intimacy, to view what Holmes obviously considered a weakness in himself.

The door opened to show the young maid, hovering on the threshold.

'Do come in, Emily, please,' said Kit firmly.

'Yes, Miss.' The barely-hidden contempt the girl had shown her in the entry hall had disappeared. Her eyes slid away from Kit's and went to the bed where Ezekiel Harrington lay. The girl's shoulders began to shake and tears welled. Kit put her arm around the maid and turned her away from the scene.

'I know it's very upsetting, Emily, but you must be brave. I'll not keep you long.'

The maid nodded, pale blue eyes blinking, but Kit could tell she was fighting the urge to look over her shoulder at the body again. 'Tell me what you found, when you came in here.'

'The first time, I brought him his hot toddy about nine after he'd gone to his room, like I always do after Mr. Peterson prepares it. I knocked and entered and put it down on the table, then I left. Later on, about half-eleven, I was on my way to bed when I saw the light under the door burning late. I thought Mr. Harrington might need something else. I knocked, like I always do, and went in. I saw them on the bed —I hadn't realized *he* was here. Mr. Peterson must have let him in.' Her lower lip trembled.

Kit asked, 'And why did you approach the bed rather than departing immediately?'

'I was going to leave, but I saw ...' the girl frowned as if trying to remember precisely. 'Neither of them was moving. Not one bit and it made me pause. Then I went over to the Master's side ...' Her trembling increased.

'How long has Milo been in Mr. Harrington's ... orbit?'

'A month, Miss,' said the maid with a lick of vitriol. Kit wished she could bottle the timbre of the girl's words; the acid could be used to etch steel or glass.

So.

'And where was Milo? On the covers or beneath?'

'On them, Miss.'

'Thank you, Emily, you may go.'

The girl dropped a hasty curtsey, threw one last look at the recumbent figure, then made for the doorway, which was suddenly filled by the bulk of Watson, Peterson and a slender youth no taller than the maid. His hair was a wispy blond that hung to his shoulders; his face was as pretty as a girl's; his clothing appeared new, albeit crumpled, as if heedlessly slept in.

The little maid hissed, 'Murderer!' and Kit feared she might strike, but then the moment was gone, the girl out in the corridor, the boy in the room, and Watson closing the door in the butler's face as Kit said, 'Thank you, Peterson.'

The boy blinked and blinked, stared around him, his gaze attaching to the body on the bed and Kit saw a terrible sadness take up residence. The full lips trembled. Kit grabbed at the boy's sharp chin and stared into his eyes.

'His pupils are pinpricks. Did you notice, Doctor?'

Watson nodded. *This time*; before they'd been too busy looking at the blood spatter. Holmes, by the window, grunted.

'I don't use it,' said the boy, tightly, his thick accent pointing to somewhere in Eastern Europe.

'Use *what*?'

The boy looked away. He wasn't really a boy, thought Kit, but a young man so fragile-looking that he seemed younger.

'You are showing signs of having used either opium or one of its by-products. You woke disoriented, did you not?'

The boy nodded slowly.

'Tell me what happened last evening,' asked Kit quietly.

'Last evening ... I arrived after nine-thirty. Ezekiel has given me a key to the back door. We have tried to be ... discreet.'

'Unsuccessfully,' sniped Holmes.

Kit gave the shadowy shape a sharp glance and there was no further comment. She sighed, and looked at the mirror over the fireplace, taking in all the inhabitants of the room, and then drew the young man to sit on the recamier.

'Please continue, Milo.'

'We spoke, then he fell asleep. And then I slept.' The boy was lying, or mixing omissions with slivers of truth. His slender hands with their long fingers were clasped in his lap, tightly interlaced.

'You said you did not use opium. But Mr. Harrington did. We have surmised it was a very recent development.' When the boy's mouth tightened, Kit hurried on, 'Milo, please trust me that your friend's reputation will suffer no more than the three of us in this room will allow; we are each here to help in our own fashion.'

Still the boy remained silent.

Kit tried a change of tack. 'Had Mr. Harrington been ill lately?'

The bottom lip trembled, then Milo nodded.

'Ezekiel has been in such pain.' He sighed. 'I have urged him to seek the advice of his physician, but he has—had—proved obdurate.'

Kit nodded. 'I've known men who'd prefer a slow death to asking for aid and thinking themselves seen as weak. Did you buy the morphine for him?'

The boy shook his head but avoided her eye; another half-truth, half-lie. He had not made the purchase, but knew who had.

'And how did you come to suffer the effects of an opiate, Milo?'

'I did not—'

Kit held up a hand. 'I do not doubt you did not take it by intent. Think on it.'

He puzzled, pale brows meeting over dark eyes. 'I drank only ... the girl brings every night a hot toddy. Ezekiel had lost his taste for it with the illness, but I found I liked it. I drank that as I have most nights here, and I slept.' Again, Kit had the sense that he was picking through the truths he knew, careful to keep others back. Giving up only what he felt he could afford to part with.

'Where's the glass?'

'On the table.' He pointed in full expectation of the object being where he'd left it, but it was not in evidence. Milo frowned, genuinely puzzled.

'Has Peterson been in here?' Kit asked.

'He said not,' Holmes answered. 'He's a stout fellow.'

'Aren't you all? And never an evasion or an untruth for the sake of honour? A devoted butler who would not gaze upon his master's death, even if only to attempt his desperate saving? Doctor, would you mind acting as my Mercury once more? Ask our erstwhile butler if he happened to fib.'

As Watson disappeared, Kit returned her attention to Milo. 'No one but Ezekiel knew that you'd taken to drinking the hot toddy?' He shook his head. 'Where did you meet Mr. Harrington?'

'On the docks.' He cleared his throat as he realized how that sounded, then amended: 'In his office. I had been a sailor, but wished for other work. I saw the sign for his office and sought him out. I can read and write, do figures, I thought perhaps to be on dry land for some while.'

Kit laughed aloud. The boy was never a sailor; oh, he might have been on a ship but that didn't make him anything more than a desperate person seeking a way out of an unpleasant life. She took his hands in hers and examined them, turned them over to caress the smooth palms; no sign of calluses or blisters, no proof of old injury such as a mariner would have experienced more than once in a life at sea. Another lie, then. The boy was running from something in his past, but probably unconnected with Ezekiel Harrington. Harrington was a new phase, a new problem, a new loss.

The door opened to reveal Watson and a shame-faced butler.

'Peterson has something to tell you.'

The butler addressed himself to Holmes. 'I'm sorry, sir. I found Mr. Harrington. I found him and didn't want him being put down as no suicide, nor dying like some stupid woman.'

'Miss Caswell asked you the question, Peterson. Do her the courtesy of answering.'

The man blushed red as a beet, but turned his gaze to Kit; his expression said he wasn't sure if he should repeat what he'd just said, as if she'd not been in the room the entire time. Kit stared at him for a long moment, then said, 'Suicide?'

'Yes, Miss. No way the Master would have taken such a cowardly way out.'

'Peterson, *how* do you think Mr. Harrington died?'

'Laudanum, Miss. I came to check on him about eleven and found him too deep asleep to wake. It became clear that he'd taken to using laudanum like the Mistress, to help him sleep.' The man looked at his shoes. 'I could smell it in the dregs of the hot toddy, Miss. Must have added it after Emily brought it up.'

'And where was Milo?'

'Asleep beside the Master.' Peterson did not look at the boy; Kit had the feeling it was not the first time over the years that the servant had seen such company in this room. 'To be honest, Miss, I thought he was dead too. I thought they'd both
...'

No, thought Kit, something was missing. There was something else he was hiding.

'Did you take the syringe and vial, Mr. Peterson?'

Startled, he stared at Kit.

'He was still alive, your master, but you feared him soon to die. Not from the laudanum but its mixing with something else ... something else you knew he had because you'd purchased it for him.'

'How can you—?'

'You're a trusted employee and I imagine you've served many years with Mr. Harrington. You knew he'd become ill, that he suffered. Where Milo refused his request for the drug, as employed servant, you had no such choice.' Kit took heart as he nodded, a sharp, shamed movement. 'I smelled the sweetness of opium smoke on you when I arrived, yet you did not strike me as a user. Ergo you'd been in a den for another purpose: seeking out a stronger solution for a man too fearful to consult his physician.' Kit clasped her hands in her lap. 'Yet when you found him deep in its grip you feared less that he had overdosed than you would be found out as having provided him with the means to do so.'

The man paled.

'Never fear, Peterson, he's no suicide. What did you do with the toddy glass?'

He blinked hard. 'Smashed it, buried the pieces in the garden. I can show you where.'

'Perhaps later. Thank you, Peterson.' Kit smiled.

'Is that all, Miss?'

'For the moment. You were cowardly, Mr. Peterson, but I do not believe you a killer.'

When the butler had shuffled from the room, Watson barely kept his oath inaudible.

'Well, Miss Caswell?' asked Holmes from the shadows.

'Peterson still thinks his master died of an overdose; he

feared that would be the outcome and lo, he assumed that the cause of death was drugs. He does not know about the knife.'

'How can that be?'

'There would be no reason for him to enter the room a second time. He believed his master to be on the way out. After Emily discovered Mr. Harrington dead, Peterson believed he knew the cause. The death was no surprise to him. Mrs. Harrington said Emily brought her news, accompanied her to this room; the lady of the house was not especially coherent, so I've no doubt she did not give any great detail. Peterson, you can see his shame. That would be enough to keep him away.'

'Then we are no closer to a solution than before you arrived, Miss Caswell.' Watson sighed.

Holmes corrected him, 'On the contrary, we know considerably more, yet this wretch continues in his refusal to confess.'

'And he is right to do so,' said Kit.

'Hello, Emily.'

'What's he doing here?' Kit had knocked and opened the door to find the maid sitting on a narrow bed, an old petticoat spread across her lap, needle and thread in her hands. Behind Kit, Holmes and Watson crowded, Milo between them.

'We can't just leave him roaming about. Never fear, Milo will be dealt with justly soon enough.' That seemed to soothe the girl's feathers. 'Darning before wash day?' asked Kit with a smile, which the girl did not bother to return as she nodded.

At the foot of the bed was a wicker laundry basket. The room was scantly furnished, but for a small set of drawers and a washstand. Kit quickly looked them over, and dismissed them. On the top of the drawers was a tiny posy of dried flowers and a few trinkets, cheap glass cleverly cut. Gifts from a suitor no doubt.

Yet it was to the basket of dirty clothes Kit gravitated, kneeling in front of the receptacle.

'Oi! You've no right to do that!' shouted the girl rather more loudly than she should.

'Caswell, that's most unsavoury and unnecessary,' Holmes said, apparently horrified at the sight of a woman's unwashed garments.

'Bachelors,' said Kit, 'are afraid of the strangest things. Remain calm, Mr. Holmes, no one is asking you to undertake washday duties.'

Kit continued to excavate the contents of the basket until at last she came to a white apron, which had been rolled into a tight bundle. Carefully she removed it and laid it on the floor, unwrapping it meticulously as if it might contain something precious.

When at last Kit was done, the apron lay open on the threadbare rug. In its middle a field of red blossoms—bloodied finger and handprints—marred the snowy fabric. 'Now, gentlemen, do you require instruction in the differences between ordinary blood and menstrual blood? This is most certainly the former.'

'Really, Miss Caswell,' Watson tutted, turning a deep crimson.

Holmes' dark eyes were fixed on her face, keen and sharp. 'Well? Tell us, you've earned the floor.'

'But the girl was with her mistress all night,' objected Watson.

'No. You merely assumed that, yet Emily herself said she'd gone to her master's room twice that evening: once to deliver his drink, the second time to check on him. And Mrs. Harrington was clearly under the influence of laudanum when

I tried to question her—Peterson told us she used it.' Kit smiled. 'She'd have no idea if the girl was there or not.'

She began to tick off points on her fingers.

'When Emily spoke of finding Mr. Harrington murdered, she said she knocked and entered. The girl is methodical in her descriptions, gentlemen: she lists each step she has undertaken. Were you to ask her how she might achieve a future task, you would discover she does the same thing as when she recalls a past action. Now, you'll recollect when she knocked on the door downstairs at my summons, she waited to be told to come in. When she described her two trips to her master's room, she did no such thing: she said she knocked and went in. That suggests to my mind at least some degree of intimacy; she knew he was in there. That on numerous other occasions she knew she did not need to await permission.'

She saw Holmes jerk in surprise. Watson hid a smile as he groomed his moustache. Kit turned to Milo.

'Were you intimate with Mr. Harrington?'

'Not in any way you might recognize, Miss.'

'When Emily spoke about this young man, she bitterly resented his intrusion into the life of the household—you've seen how she reacts to his presence—but at no point has she mentioned her poor mistress as his "victim". As if Mrs. Harrington was not the one displaced. That suggested to me that she cared not a jot for the position of the lady of the house.'

One more finger was tapped.

'The direction of the cut on Mr. Harrington's throat could only have been made by someone standing to his right— if that had been Milo there would have been blood spray on the covers. Yet he lay there creating a void and you'll note, if you look carefully, the dark patches on his jacket where the blood spurted. He could not have been the murderer.'

One last finger was folded away.

'And I could not help but question what maid has such a pristine apron on after midnight?' Kit tilted her head as she surveyed the girl who sat so very still on the bed. 'Unless she didn't want anyone to see what she'd wiped on it. Emily, why?'

'Because once he met *that* he never looked at me again! Not once.' The girl began to sob, angry gasps not sad ones, rage at being caught. 'I looked after him! Me! I was the one he looked to for comfort. Then this thing came and turned his head and heart. After all our time together, after all the lovely gifts he gave me.' She threw a hand towards the pile of cheaply glittering trinkets.

'You cared for him. You brought him the hot toddy every evening. You knew he'd been in pain ...'

Emily nodded. 'I put some of the mistress's laudanum in it last night, to help.'

'But he'd stopped drinking it.'

'Didn't know that, did I? But then I found *them* asleep together. Him'—she glared at Milo—'in *my* spot, laying where I used to, ought to. And I thought how Ezekiel threw me aside so easily and what if I killed two birds with one stone? Revenge on both of them, the one for casting me away, the other for taking my place.'

'And of course you'd had the foresight to take one of the silver letter openers with you from Mr. Harrington's desk earlier,' said Kit smoothly.

The maid jerked back as if slapped by proof of her obvious premeditation.

'And so.' Kit sighed and re-wrapped the apron, then stood, and handed the bundle to Watson. 'Perhaps now would be the time to send for the police. I'm sure you can explain it adequately, gentlemen. As I am rather unpopular with the Met in general and Inspector Makepeace in particular, I think it best if I depart.'

'Miss Caswell—'

'Mr. Holmes, I suggest you allow this young man his liberty. I do not believe he will do well under another round of questioning from the peelers. Milo? Perhaps will you be so good as to escort me?'

Downstairs, Kit found that Peterson had acquired a hansom cab; she shooed Milo ahead of her.

Kit bade farewell to the good doctor. 'Good evening, Doctor Watson. I feel almost sorry that I was unable to find anything more in Heaven and Earth for you.'

He smiled, relieved.

Holmes led her down the front stairs, and before she could climb into the cab he grasped her hand. 'Thank you, Miss Caswell. You have delivered a salutary lesson in observation.' Then he leaned in close and whispered almost beseechingly, 'That boy. There's something odd about that boy, isn't there?'

Kit nodded slowly. 'Do you want to know what it is? I warn you, sir, it's not rational and will not fit well in your view of the universe.'

There was a long hesitation before Holmes shook his head and gave a rueful smile. 'A man must know his limitations, Miss Caswell.'

He helped her into the cab, then waited on the footpath to watch as the vehicle rattled away.

Inside the cool dimness of the cab, faces occasionally lit by the streetlamps they passed, Kit and Milo sat in silence for several minutes, until Milo said tentatively, 'When ... when did you know?'

'In the bedroom.'

'When both Peterson and Emily said they thought I no longer breathed?'

She laughed. 'No. They both said you did not *move*; neither mentioned breath. It was when I noticed you had no reflection in the mirror above the fireplace.'

He gave a chuckle of comprehension. 'That was why you moved me away from it, yes?'

She nodded. 'I have read about your kind, Milo—do you have a last name?'

'Albescu. My true name is Sorin Albescu, but I am Milo to this world.'

'Aha! Well, Mr. Albescu, I am aware of your kind.'

'And yet you've put yourself in close proximity with me? Are you not afraid, Miss Caswell?'

'Only a fool would hurt me when we were last seen together by the World's Greatest Detective and the World's Most Devoted Physician. Is my instinct that you're not a killer wrong?' Kit slid her hand into her reticule and grasped the handle of the remaining silver letter opener which she'd 'souvenired' before she left from Ezekiel Harrington's desk in case of just such an exigency. Silver was one of the things that sources seemed to agree on as a *deterrent* to the undead.

'You will know, if you have done your research, that my kind must feed. I feed, yet I have never killed. I do not begin a *relationship* with an unwilling partner, Miss Caswell. I fed on Ezekiel last night as I have every time since I met him.'

Kit slapped her knee. 'Of course! The marks on his thigh —there seemed too many for one night's injection site.'

'It was easy to camouflage the needle pricks amongst the marks of my teeth, they are very similar. Our intercourse was not sexual, at least not as you might understand. He was my friend. He gave me shelter—rented rooms for me where I might safely sleep during the day—and in return ...'

'Did he think your kiss, your bite might save him?'

Milo nodded in the brief light. 'I tried to explain that what I have—what I *am*—is not a gift. That my immortality was not of my choosing. That the price was and has always been too high.'

'Desperation will make people refuse to see what is in front of them.' Kit sighed.

'That was his tragedy—and mine—to have met when he was at his most needy, his most vulnerable. What might we have had in other circumstances?' Milo asked wistfully.

'If I'm to let you go in this city, what will you do? Propagate?'

'That has never been my way, Miss Caswell.' He smiled and it seemed impossibly bright in the dimness of the cab. 'A creature who lives like that—who does murder and makes others like itself—will soon be found out.' He gave a sigh containing untold centuries of regret. 'We are but scraps and echoes, Miss Caswell, things that have fallen from humanity, but remember our old shape too well to let it go entirely. I would not condemn anyone else to this life.'

All she'd read suggested beings like Milo were soulless, yet she'd seen nothing in the past hours to support that. Kit took a deep breath. 'Then you'd best go. The sun will not be kind to you, will it?'

'The matter of light is a constant for the living and the undead.'

'If you ever need help, Mr. Albescu, seek me out.'

'Thus I will say the same to you, Miss Caswell. I thank you for this evening's kindness.' He bent over her hand and she felt only the touch of his cold, cold lips; no breath escaped them. Then he was gone, the door of the cab opening and closing with terrible swiftness, and Kit was alone.

How you viewed life was, she reflected, all a matter of light.

WHEN WE FALL, WE FORGET

The mist beyond the low stone wall is thick, now white, now grey, sometimes shading to a black that blends with the night, so it's hard to tell where one begins and the other ends. Never seen anything quite like it, though I've travelled far, but this is different from any place I've ever been. Insular people, the small distances between their holdings might as well be a hundred miles for all the interest they take in their neighbours —unless there are secrets in the offing, and even then. The little town that clings to the earth sloping down to the harbour is not quite so bad; something to do, I suppose, with being in close proximity, the necessity of human contact. And they all go to one church or the other, depending upon their own version of God and Its message. There's a tidy white-washed Protestant place of worship in town, a grey stone Catholic one about ten minutes out of it. The name of this island doesn't matter; it's much like the one where my memories began and ended, those left to me along with my troubles.

I've been sitting on the front stoop for too long, the cold

has numbed my backside and legs, made my lower back ache, but I don't get up. Mortal hurts still strike me as novel even after all these years. The sun sank while I sat here, hands wrapped around a cup of tea that cooled far too soon, and the fog began in the peat bogs just on the other side of the road that hardly anyone drives down anymore now they're used to me. My cardigan's too thin. If I had any sense I'd have gone in long ago, tended the hearth, had blazes crackling in the sitting room and in the upstairs bedroom I've chosen—I prefer the fireplaces to the rattling radiators, prefer the true warmth, the ancient warmth. But I am watching the mist as I do every evening, watching it mass above the bogs, creep up and over the road, then press and froth at the low stone wall that encloses my garden. Each night it creaks and clatters the rickety wooden gate, but it never pushes through, not even spilling between the long gaps from paling to paling. As if whatever waits out there keeps it at bay.

Ariel would have liked it here, the way the house is so close to the cliff, overlooking the sea. The rush and roar and crash of the waves on the rocks below, how the sound of it is constant. I'd have had to watch her, though, so close to the edge; the thing is, we'd not have been here had I not lost her once before.

The house crouches behind me, breathes over my shoulder. The place was already furnished, mostly antiques, not necessarily comfortable, but I make do. I need so little. It has three storeys: on the ground floor a kitchen, a library, a sitting room; upstairs four bedrooms and a renovated bathroom. Above that the tiny, airless attic with dust on the floorboards and a round window of red, blue and green, small enough for a child to push her head through should the mood take. Sometimes I hear what might be footsteps up there, the echoing sighs of forgotten things.

A racket at the gate catches my attention. The mist is shifting, spinning as if it might form into something new, something tall with substance. It brushes against the wooden entrance, shakes it enough to produce a noise that might hide a moan or a groan or even the sweep of a sharp metal object through the air. It struggles, wavers, fails, and falls away. It's not time yet; there are more tasks to be done.

I force myself upwards. My knees protest. I arch backwards and feel the little cracks as each vertebra returns to its proper alignment. Sighing, I turn and go inside, closing the door behind me. There are things that need doing, and this body must sleep.

At mid-afternoon the sun's made half an effort, and though the light is mostly grey there are some shades of gold to it, here and there. The wind alternates between sly nips and outright bites. You can see why the trees, cut down in ancient times, were reluctant to grow again. There are only a few stunted oaks across the island, like the one clinging drunkenly to the side of the granite church. An angry tenuous tree, ugly and twisted, refusing to go without a fight. I imagine how my daughter would have squealed with delight to see it, to climb it, to perch triumphantly in branches not too far from the ground.

There's no warmth, though. I settle the knitted cap more firmly on my hair so the breeze can't pluck the red locks away, hunch my shoulders, jam my hands back into the pockets of my puffer jacket, and continue towards the church and the small rectory beside it which houses the local priest.

As I get closer the stained-glass windows seem to glow. I shake my head. *Lighting inside the building*. Nothing to be afraid of. I smile: it's so long since I've felt fear the sensation is strange. The glasswork is very fine and I shouldn't be surprised, I suppose. The Faithful always want the best for their houses of worship no matter how remote, will always empty their pockets, go short, starve their own children, if only the structure where they think God resides might be magnificent in some way. As if It's not got better places to be.

The glass angels are exquisite, however, kind and forgiving, strikingly lovely as they deliver tidings of comfort and joy, and lambs to and from slaughter. I'm not sure what I feel as I look at them, whether I hear the singing of metal again, the sound Ramiel told me was the last I ever heard.

Off to my right are ranks of peat bricks and the earth they've been dug from. They lie like soldiers, waiting. Soon they'll be stacked, herringboned, to dry. No one's around.

As with every other dwelling here, a low stone wall marks out the boundaries. Inside the graveyard are headstones, the older ones covered in mosses from deep fern green to almost lime then to a seafoam hue. Many of the names have been weathered away. I focus on the double doors; oak, I think, presumably brought over from the mainland where trees are plentiful, stained by age, smoothed by years of priestly and penitential hands, by the dogged ministrations of the ever-present wind. The lock, if ever it was polished to a shine, is black now. The left panel hangs ajar, but the sunlight doesn't creep too far inside.

I take a deep breath and move along the path, through the gap in the wall. Nothing happens, no bolt of lightning, no thunder, the sky does not split. I keep walking, right up to the doors, and there is only a tiny tremor in my fingers when I push them open. As I step over the threshold that spot between my shoulder blades begins to itch.

It takes a while for my eyes to adjust to the darkness of the tiny porch, and I bump my hip against something hard: a marble font, carved like a gigantic cup with hands wrapped around the rim. The water within shimmers darkly and I don't dip into it, don't cross myself and hope for the best like others. My reflection in it is an uncertain thing. There are rows of pews in the nave, twenty each to the left and right, on either side of an aisle of flagstones that have also served as headstones for those who've been judged as good and great. At the far end flicker many points of light: candelabras ranged on both sides of a small altar, and in front of that altar with its white gold-embroidered cloth and carven tabernacle, is a man in a black cassock, turned towards me. He's like a shadow against the pristine fabric.

A man who gasps as I step from the gloom.

What does he *see*?

He puts out a hand to steady himself, the other comes up as if to ward me off. I smile. The doors behind me swing properly shut, cutting off the watery daylight that's made me a silhouette to him.

'Father McBride?'

I can hear his breathing, it's slowing, calming as he sees me for a human being after all. He nods, trying to collect himself.

What did he see?

'I'm Sarai McEwan.'

'Ah. The new girl at the big house on the Old Road.' And he smiles as if that might cover the fact he was terribly afraid for however brief a time. That I might be reduced to a series of descriptors. *Girl.* Trying to make me small, unimportant to make himself feel big again. Once upon a time I'd have given him a lecture about infantilising women, but there are more important matters.

'Not so new,' is what I say instead. 'Mhairead Spence at the historical society said I might chat with you.'

'I'll speak to any who come to me in need,' he says and I

sense a homily approaching. I feel the heat of angry blood flooding my face, have to work hard to keep my voice steady. I think how it could all be done with now, that I could take up a candlestick or that fine shiny monstrance and ... but no. There's an order to things, steps that need following if I'm to get my wish.

'How kind. But it's not your godliness I'm in need of today, Father.' I barely keep the contempt from my tone. 'But your archaeological knowledge, that's another thing entirely.'

His expression flickers like slides onto a screen, one change after another, subtlety different until it settles to a kindly frown. Registering the rejection of one thing and the offering of another, unexpected thing. There's uncertainty, too; his past clings to him as surely as a phantom limb. Doesn't everyone's?

'That's a long time ago, Miss McEwan.'

'You're not that old,' I say; flattery works even on a priest, I can see it in his face as I draw closer. Especially on a priest. He's in his forties, perhaps closer to fifty than not, but he's handsome, square jaw, features rugged as if carved by his time on this island, and eyes the pale shade of blue I associate with a stript soul, with heartache, with a loss that's leeched part of your very life from you. Eyes like my own. He's tall, bulky, would turn to fat quickly if he weren't careful, going for a run at dawn and dusk, past my house, muscular arms and legs pumping, fighting off whatever cold might try to get into his bones; he's been here so long, the climate shouldn't both him anymore. The thick, salt and pepper hair is longer and untidier than seemly for a man of his profession and vintage, but I don't imagine the spinsters and widows who come to listen to his preaching mind so terribly much; nor the married women and some of the men.

'I don't know much about the house where I'm staying, you see, just that an adventurer built it and filled it with his souvenirs.' I smile again, take the last few steps and offer my hand. After a moment, he accepts; his skin is warm, rough with calluses from years of digging that no amount of time will smooth away. His pupils dilate at the touch. I don't look my age, and my lips are full, my eyes slanted, full-lashed; all the tales I've heard say that Gunn McBride always did have an eye for a beautiful woman. No reason why that would have changed just because he found God.

'Thomas Earnchester, one of those Englishmen with too much money and a fascination with things that didn't concern him. He died without heirs, and left the estate to the Free Church. Everything's been gradually sold off until only the house remains, and they let that out as a holiday rental.'

'There you go, Mrs Spence was right,' I say. 'You're very well informed.'

He shrugs. 'I've been here the better part of twenty years. A body picks up bits and pieces of rumours and tales.'

'There's a mummy,' I tell him, and he tilts his head, arctic gaze narrowing. 'In a glass case.'

'I've never heard of it,' he says as if he should have.

I ask casually, 'Have you visited there before?'

He shakes his head.

Good.

'It was up in the attic. I was exploring, that's how I found it. Her. It. It's not terribly big so I moved her to the sitting room.' I pull the knitted cap from my head, and curls tumble out, catching the light from the candles; his eyes follow the fall. 'A peat mummy, I think, judging by the tea colour of the skin, but I'm no expert.'

He nods. 'The constitution of the bogs does that. Depending on the acid concentration in the water, it will either eat the bones away and leave the skin and hair, or strip away the flesh and skin and leave the bones. They tend towards the former here.'

'Will you come and look? Please? Mhairead said you'd been an archaeologist once, that you'd know best. Only I feel it should be better looked after, not just gathering dust like some old fake mermaid sewn together by carnival shysters. If it's valuable, it should go to a museum, but I don't want to trouble anyone unless ...'

He smiles and I know what he's thinking: *Don't want to trouble anyone but me.* I smile back, thinking *What else are you doing with your time?*

'Besides, I'd be happy of the company if only for a little while,' I say, fully aware of the power of a woman's attention, even on a priest. Especially on a priest.

'Tomorrow afternoon, then,' he says and I release a breath. 'I've evening mass and community visits to make tonight. I don't imagine your girl's in any great hurry.'

'Tomorrow afternoon will be perfect,' I say, though my pulse seems loud in my temples. My girl's waited a long time; what's one more day? My heart aches at the delay. I release his hand at last, feel the sudden cold. 'I look forward to it.'

I hesitate a little longer, stare at the stained-glass windows once more, at the beatific faces that might or might not be familiar. Feel the itch between my shoulder blades again. Feel a similar itch at the back of my memory where the forgotten things wait.

'Anything else I can do for you, Ms McEwan?' he asks and his voice is soft, so soft it might contain an invitation.

I give another smile, a brilliant thing. 'Just admiring your angels, Father, they're lovely.'

He looks at them as if for the first time. 'They're doing their duty, it makes them beautiful.'

I laugh. 'Oh, Father, the fallen are lovely too, and don't you forget it. Didn't Lucifer keep his good looks? Otherwise how might he tempt righteous souls?'

I walk towards home faster than I left it. Almost there, I

have to pause at the side of the road until the shaking rage passes. I don't throw up, though I felt I might. I straighten, take in the height, the breadth, the many stones that went into the house's makeup. I look up at the attic window and think I see a shape pressed against the glass, but I know nothing's there, not really. Just a sliver, a memory, a shade. Not a whole thing, not yet.

The night drags on. When I finally sleep, I dream of wings and old things that were given up, sacrificed. I dream of the things I yearned for, the things I got, and then lost. I wake in the dark hours to the certainty that someone is in the room, but when I open my eyes no one is there. Tiptoeing to the window, I peer out the sliver between the thick curtains.

Outside the low stone wall the fog roils, agitates, rebels, but does not enter the garden.

'Did you speak to him, love?' Mhairead Spence had asked when I ran into her in the village store.

I stocked up on coffee and biscuits, which is basically what I exist on, and she on items far more appropriate, like fresh fruit and vegetables, flour and tea. 'Thank you, Mrs Spence.'

She nodded, a housewifely gesture, pleased that matters have gone as she'd expected. 'He's good man for all he's a Catholic. I've always thought him a little haunted.'

'Ah, Mrs Spence, we drag our ghosts behind us whether we want to or not.'

'You've an old head on you.' *She's got no idea*. 'Have a lovely evening, Sarai.'

'And you, Mrs Spence,' I'd said and watched her bustle her groceries up to the counter.

Now I press my fingers against the pane, feel it cold despite the double-glazing. The fire in the hearth has gone out and the chill is palpable. Down below one of my ghosts waits, stoic, with the patience of a statue. Eventually I go back to bed and find a dreamless slumber awaits.

'She's a lovely thing,' Father Gunn McBride says, crouching in front of the case, two fingers resting against the glass as if to steady his balance. His eyes are avid, almost warm with interest.

The little tea-brown girl lies on a bed of dirt, her head and shoulders twisted one way, the rest of her body the other, as if she was shifted and warped in the earth's damp embrace. The long plaits are a bright ochre red; once they were golden, but the bog had changed them too. The acid of the water has eaten away most of her clothing, so it's not likely he'll recognise that as an anachronism. And there's that strange sheen to the skin; that and the colour of her, the distortion of her features from the pressure of liquid and peat, make her unrecognisable except to one who loved her.

'Exquisite in death, isn't she? I think you've got a prize here, Ms McEwan.'

'Sarai, please.'

'Then I'm Gunn,' he says and smiles. 'Of course, she'll need to be x-rayed, all the usual tests conducted to make sure she's what she appears. I can put you in contact with some people at one of the universities on the mainland. I'm sure they'll be keen to help. I imagine the letting agent will want to be notified, though.'

'I'll tell her,' I say. 'Can I interest you in a drink? Sherry?'

'What do you take me for? A reverend?' He laughs as he says it.

'Whiskey then?'

'No alcohol for me, thank you.' Yet there's longing in his eyes, a whisper of it in his tone. Gunn McBride used to love his booze just as he loved his beautiful women. Probably more, and that's where he came apart.

'I wonder where she's from?' His voice is quite soft, musing. He sounds oddly kind and tender, as if he feels some responsibility for her, which he should. 'I wonder what happened to her? A sacrifice, do you think? I can't see a garrotte around her neck, nor any obvious stab wounds. Perhaps poison or blow to the back of the head?'

I wonder that he can discuss the death of a girl so casually, I turn away so he can't see my face. 'I'll make tea, then.'

When we're settled in the sitting room, the fire crackling merrily, the glass case between us, I say, 'May I ask a question, Father?'

'You just did,' he says and chuckles as if it's terribly funny. I want to tell him it's not, but I just smile. 'Of course you may, Sarai. And it's Gunn, don't forget,' as if his name is an intimacy he can force upon me.

'What did you see? When I walked into the church yesterday?' I sip at my own beverage, a dash of whiskey to fortify it.

His gaze slides away, latches onto the flames in the hearth, is held there for a few beats too long, then he lamely produces, 'A trick of the light was all,' and says no more.

We sit in silence for a while, drinking, looking anywhere but at each other, until he breaks at last. 'And what about you, Sarai? What do you do? What brings you to us?'

'I travel,' I answer and smile. 'I read, I research, sometimes I write. I witness and I watch, and if I can I set things to rights.'

'Independently wealthy and aimless, then?' He misunderstands, of course, though he can't know it. 'Nice thing to be.'

'It costs me sure enough, Gunn,' I use his name and see

him blink. 'And I only appear aimless to those who don't pay enough attention.'

His gaze moves once again, to something behind me, or that he thinks is there. The stare traces an outline I can only imagine. 'And you, Gunn, what made you change? From archaeologist to shepherd?'

It takes an effort for him to refocus, and his grin is uncomfortable.

'Mid-life crisis, shall we say? I found I had insufficient faith to support the life I was living. I needed something else, something that didn't come at the bottom of a bottle or beneath a short skirt.' He shakes his head as if hit by the confessional urge. 'Life was easy for me, Sarai. Things came easily to me, jobs, successes, women, and I let them go just as easily because I didn't value them. I assumed that something new would replace whatever slid away. For a long time I was right; and then ... then came a hole so deep I couldn't fill it not matter what I poured down my throat or snorted up my nose or stuck my cock in.' His gaze flits to see if that shocks me; I wonder how often he's given this speech, if it's a standard he pulls out when trying to convince someone of his sincerity. I might have believed him, too, if not for that little glance. if I didn't know what he'll never actually confess.

'And you found what you needed in a black robe, performative cannibalism, and the fairy story of a dead god come back to life?' I raise my cup as if in toast, see his flare of annoyance—not panic, too arrogant for that—to realise I've not fallen for his act.

'Will you look at the hour, Ms McEwan? Time for me to go.' He goes to put his cup on the coffee table and misses. The delicate vessel falls to the carpet, doesn't smash, but the remnants of dark bitter liquid soak into the weave. He's apologetic, embarrassed. 'I'm sorry, how clumsy of me! I must have misjudged ...'

'Nothing to apologise for, Father McBride. No harm done. Just leave it.' I crouch in front of him, right the cup and put it on the table, then take his hands and rise, pulling him with me. We stand so close I can feel his breath on my face. He stares at me. I let one hand drop, turn and lead him behind me. His feet seem to drag when we pass the stairs that go up, but I don't pause. I guide him to the front door, open it, and let his hand go. His fingers dance across my palm and he wavers on the stoop as if I might change my mind.

'For all you've found God, you don't always want him around, do you?' I breathe into his face, all whiskey and sugar sweetness, and I can see it excites him. I think about the core of him, that he sometimes fights, but eventually gives in to. There's too much of him that favours the darkness. And I want to put my hands around his thick throat and squeeze.

But I don't.

I push him away, out into the night. He staggers a little down the steps, watches me close the door ever so slowly. I don't know how long he'll stay out there. But he'll be back, I do know that much.

Once upon a time, Gunn McBride hid after he did what he did. He hid the result of his careless act and avoided the consequences. He hid from himself, from his conscience, pretended to find salvation in a new life. But it's all a façade, all a dream, all make-believe. It's just for *show*.

Two days and he doesn't return.

Two days and I think I've lost him.

Two days and I fear he's fled. I'll have to trace him, track him, stalk him. Hunt him. As if I haven't done that enough all these years.

Was I overconfident? Have I lost my chance? What if he sensed something? What if, when given the choice, he elected not to descend? Not to seal his own fate? What if he's been genuine in his repentance? For long moments I'm convinced I don't have the energy to pursue him anymore. That it will be easier, simpler to just let him go. To forgive if not to forget.

Then I remind myself what I would be giving up. What I already gave up *before*. I remind myself that was enough, if not too much, that I will not surrender this. I will not abandon her. I will not fail her again.

And in that darkness sitting vigil over the glass coffin, in that deepest pit of anguish, when what passes for my soul kindles and reaches, when I recall the determination that's kept me going, the doorbell rings.

There are shadows under his eyes, he's forgone the cassock, is in his running gear, perspiration pouring off him despite the chill air. I wonder if he's been drinking; I can smell the stale sweat with a hint of barley. Fallen off the wagon into the whiskey vat.

I'm pulling the door open as he's pushing it, then he's on me and soon in me, and I don't care. This act is needed to show his fall is entire, that he's not true to the life he claims. That he's faithless.

And for me there's relief in the physical contact, in the animal nature of the act, in knowing I've not lost. Who'd begrudge me that small comfort? I run my nails down his back, digging furrows that draw grunts from him but don't slow him down. Then I'm on top of him and his eyes widen, go to a point behind my shoulders, and I hiss, 'What do you see?'

This time he answers, gasping, 'Wings. Wings!' and reaches up to touch them, to outline their feathery tips, but I know he won't be able to make contact, that they're not really there. Just ghostly things clinging to my back like cobwebs, impossible to shift, to leave behind. 'How can you have these? Have I gone mad?'

'No more than the rest of us, Father,' I laugh, moving against him until he's caught once again in what we're doing and forgets to ask questions for a while.

When we're done and lying on the hall rug, he runs his fingers across the skin of my back as if he might feel what he can no longer see, and asks, 'What are you? One of *them*?'

'Once, so I've been told. No longer.'

'Do you not know?'

'When we fall, we forget. Our wings are taken, sliced away with a great scythe, and our memories of our time aloft are removed, too.'

'Then how ...'

'Writings.' I sigh. 'And those who remain Above, who are not Fallen, they come to us. When we despair, they give us tasks, offer hope that perhaps we might one day find grace again if we are obedient.'

'But if you can't remember then how do you know they're not demons tempting you? That you're not ... ?'

'Mad? I've asked myself that time and again, especially when the one who came to me first appeared. I can't remember, but I feel these.' I point to the wings that are both there and not there. 'They make us promises, that we can earn back what we lost. Most of us want our wings returned, having discovered the things for which we fell not worth the sacrifice.'

'And you? What did you lose?' he asks tenderly and I can almost believe he's genuine. But I think of how casually he spoke of my girl's death, thinking her an ancient sacrifice, how he never confessed to his deed not even to another priest in the sanctity of confessional.

'Her. I'm told I chose to fall so I could have her. I'm told I questioned our nature, demanded to know why we did so little beyond fetching and carrying; why we created so little, why nothing we did was *generative*.' I shake my head. 'Some days I wonder if I *do* remember: if there are cracks in the world, between what was and what is, if my memories are bleeding through.' I raise a hand as if I might catch at something, at a truth, then sigh again. 'Yet really I remember nothing but her, and that's because she came after I fell. I chose to be human so I could have her. All I ever wanted was a child; it must have been what I wanted because that desire was the only thing I could recall the day I awoke, wingless. I found a man who was kind. I conceived, nothing miraculous in that. I had her, my little one, my tiny joy. I had her for eight years.' I shrug as if it were all so simple, as if the time passed as easily as I've made the tale sound.

He says nothing, just watches my face. No sign from him that he recognises any of this story, no sign of compassion or even fleeting discomfort to hear of the death of a girl-child.

'Surely I knew from *before* that nothing lasts, that you mortals are so ephemeral—surely that piece of knowledge would have stuck—but I had her and thought she'd be there forever.' I smile, but there's no warmth in it. 'It's hard for angels to understand precisely how fragile life is. That humans are God's goldfish, pretty, circling, soon to be dead and flushed.'

'What happened?' he asks, still stroking me. His touch raises goosebumps or perhaps it's just this part of the telling.

'A man killed her, a bright young man, an archaeologist on a dig. A drunk on an island not so terribly different to this one —he didn't know me, didn't know my child, it was purely coincidental. Hit her as she rode her bicycle home from school. Hit her and hurt her and instead of calling for help and taking the consequences, he feared for his reputation, his career.' He's gone terribly still his fingers frozen in the small of my back. 'He was too drunk to slow down, too drunk to avoid hitting my Ariel, but sober enough to think to hide her body in the peat bog not far from the road. Sober enough to know she'd turn to a sack of leathery skin with her bones eaten away by the acid of the mire, that given enough time she'd look like an ancient mummy, a sacrifice from long ago.'

I sit up and lean against the wall, nesting amongst our discarded clothes. It's cold here, but I don't care: the chill reminds me I'm alive. That I *feel*. His face hangs as if all the muscles have been cut.

'How can you know?' he manages. 'I told no one. Not ever...'

'You didn't need to. You can't hide from the angels. God perhaps—It's very busy, gets distracted—but the angels ... well, their job is to watch and they're terribly good at that.' I lean forward, push a stray strand of hair out of his pale blue eyes. '*His* name is Ramiel, the one who came to me, and we were siblings, or so he says. He has dominion over those who rise from the dead. God lets us go if we ask, but It doesn't like to, not really—doesn't like losing souls any more than your Church does. So, when the chance comes to bring one back to the fold ...'

'I didn't mean it.'

'It took me so long to find her. Too long. There was nothing that could be done, the skeleton was gone, she's just a piece of old leather now, my little girl. Or, more correctly, she was broken into a trinity: the body, the ghost that waits upstairs, and the soul that lives in the mists outside, waiting.' I wipe away my tears. 'Some just want to take their place amongst the heavenly host once more. But I couldn't have cared less about that, about the wings. Ramiel didn't come to me until I despaired, didn't offer anything until I was in a place where I'd do anything to get my daughter back.'

I lean forward. 'And I have done so much to earn my reward, Father McBride. I have hunted so many evil-doers, so many sinners whose very existence is anathema to the godhead. I have been the instrument of punishment for so many years since you killed my Ariel, but finally I am told I have earned my reward.'

'I didn't mean it,' he says again, plaintive as a boy who feels he's wrongly punished, struggling upwards to pull his shorts back on, his shirt over his sweating torso. But he doesn't run, doesn't break for the door, as if needing the end of the story keeps him rooted. 'I didn't mean it, Sarai. I'm sorry. I was a different man, then, fearful of my freedom, my reputation.'

'And yet you never came forward. You hid in the priesthood as if you were somehow absolved, as if prayers and lip service might set you free of all your sins. You never spoke what you'd done, not even in the confessional booth.' I look at him, pitiless, and say, 'It doesn't matter. Whether you meant it or not, you did it. And you tried to hide it. Her. You *did* hide her. My little one, my love.'

And I can see in his eyes how I look. I wonder if I appeared like that when I had wings, when, Ramiel had told me, I made judgments and handed down wisdoms and punishments.

'What will happen to me? What do you want?'

'Ah, you've made your own choices, taken your own steps, which is why I've not killed you myself.' I rise. 'It's time for you to leave. Away with you, then.' I open the door, feeling the wind lick at my bare skin; I point out to the terribly thick fog that dances just beyond the gate. 'That's the way you need to go.'

And he nods, befuddled and drunk on all that's happened, all he's learned, all that's been taken from him even as it's been given; drunk on the idea that he's escaped consequences one more time. He walks with an assurance that surprises and angers me. He doesn't notice even as he goes out the garden gate the creature in the mist, the one with wings such as I once had. Ramiel doesn't follow him, doesn't need to, just waits as do I.

Waits for Gunn McBride's feet to take the trail that's

irrevocably changed, that no longer goes towards his church and the tiny rectory beside it where he'd be warm and safe and comfortable. We linger expectantly, Ramiel and I, in the terrible cold until we hear the trickle of falling rocks, then a cry from Father McBride's lips, a single sharp sound that breaks over my ears like shattered glass, and sets everything in motion.

I looked towards the fog that takes a shape that is *not* Ramiel who has dominion over those who rise, but another, smaller form that shudders and shivers as if it too has wings or is being birthed. I feel a sympathetic tremor on my bare shoulder blades. A stream of mist breaks through the gate palings and shoots its way up the path, past me with the coldest breath of air, and into the sitting room where the display case lies. From the attic comes a cry and a shape, pale and elongated, flowing to the case just as the mist comes in the door.

I scramble to follow, watch as it finds its way into the casket through cracks and crevices invisible to the naked eye. The glass is icy beneath my fingertips as I flick the hidden latch and lift the lid. The vapour pours into the holes in my daughter's body, up nostrils, into parted lips, and seashell-curved ears. She slips inside herself once again, into her skin, into that empty shell I've carted from place to place for so long. She reaches for me, mouths *Mama*, as though she's no voice left to her, as though it's yet to return.

Ariel's warm and soft, her skin growing paler by the second, her limbs firmer as the bones are reinstated, as her head and face lay claim once more to a pleasing, recognisable shape. I can smell the vinegary whiff of the acid that preserved her and hid her so no one but those who watch would know what Gunn McBride had done. So I wouldn't know where she'd gone until Ramiel at last decided it was my time, and told me where to look. Told me what I had to do to get her back, to earn her resurrection from the angel of those who rise; and I never questioned him, simply obeyed.

And here she is at last, breathing once again, and I feel as if each breath goes some way to filling all the absences in my life. My child, all I wanted, all I needed. Whatever memories were taken when the great scythe removed my wings have no value beside this restoration. I know one thing with utter certainty: that my daughter was a worthy reason to fall.

NEW WINE

'If you leave that dish on the table instead of rinsing it and putting it in the dishwasher, I will make you miserable for a week.'

Valerie's voice floats back to him from the entry hall of the too-big house; she's gone to collect the mail. There's the click of her returning heels on the parquet floors, coming closer.

'But it's my birthday!' Alek, bag over his shoulder, having just risen, is two and a half steps away from the kitchen table (where they eat in preference to the formal dining room).

'I don't care,' she sings back.

He turns around, grabs the cereal bowl, and does what he should have done in the first place. He makes noise while he does it so she'll hear.

'Yes, Valerie.' *How the hell does she do that?* Two years, almost, and he still hasn't figured it out. Every damned time. Maybe it's just because she observes him at close quarters; Alek wonders sometimes if she pays extra attention to one child because she once failed to do so to another.

Alek likes his tutor, he really does. Although that's a weirdly small word for what she does: keeping him on top of his studies and doing well, managing the occasional day staff at the house (cleaners, gardener, repairmen), feeding them both, generally ensuring he stayed out of trouble. And that was how his dad pitched the job to her: *Tutor my boy.* But the surrogate mom stuff? That kind of took them both by surprise, Alek thinks, but maybe they're good for each other. Everyone in Mercy's Brook knows what happened with Valerie's daughter, but that's the reason Valerie came into Alek's life and some days he finds it hard to feel bad about it.

Valerie in her sunflower summer dress appears in the kitchen doorway as Alek is closing the dishwasher; he waves his hands *ta-dah!*

'Lordy, don't you deserve a parade?' She smiles to take out the sting, and it's the brightest thing. Alek remembers his father Reid saying that most of the guys in their high school class had a crush on her, Reid included—almost all unrequited. From what Alek's seen of the stares from middle-aged men when he helps her do the groceries that hasn't changed much, and a lot of his own college friends aren't immune to her either, no matter that she's old enough to be their mom.

'Late lecture tonight?' she asks.

'Yeah.'

He likes that she thinks he's smart. *Knows* he's smart. He even likes that she understands how lazy he can be, but she just crosses her arms and stares at him with those hazel eyes until he pulls his head out of his ass and does the work. She's smart too, so smart it kind of scares him a little. Okay, a lot, but he likes having her around. Her sense of humor is so dry sometimes it almost chokes him. She knows him and seems to like him anyway. Sometimes he thinks he's lazy for attention or it's just to make sure his dad keeps her around longer. Truth is, Alek stays more or less on the straight and narrow when she's there because he doesn't want to disappoint her, not totally, and Alek's dad—who travels a lot—is fine with that. Ultimately the costs of a live-in tutor are nothing compared to boot camp, rehab and lawyers' fees.

As he passes by he kisses on her on the cheek, which he sometimes does, and gruffly says, 'Bye.'

The walls of the hallway leading to the front door are hung with a variety of antique mirrors. Alek's spent much of his life hating the things because looking in them was the most alone he ever felt. There were days he wasn't sure he was even there. In the past there had been days when he thought he could see through himself, through the reflection. But since Valerie'd come to stay, he's felt solid. He can live with the mirrors. Alek doesn't want to go back to looking through himself again. Valerie *sees* him; she gives him weight.

'Chocolate cake?' she calls after him.

'Extra frosting?' He grins but doesn't turn around. It's his birthday, but with his father away—Reid's always away with his IT business—and a big party planned for the weekend, it'll be just them tonight.

'Of course.'

Valerie supposes that having had a daughter, once, makes it easier to care about the boy, which sometimes strikes her as strange because when Lily disappeared Valerie stopped caring about anyone for a long time. Especially when she realized all those well-meaning, fuck-all-doing cops who patted her shoulder and told her they'd do their best, just went back to eat their way through a truck-load of donuts. Her ex-husband was just as useless.

Briefly she flips through the bundle of mail. There's a bunch of bills. A rectangle of pink addressed to Alek, and redolent of perfume that no doubt has some starlet's name attached to it and turns into a cat's piss stench after five minutes on the skin. The plain white envelope is the only one addressed to her, and in a very distinctive hand that makes her sigh. She feels the weight of the house overhead: two floors above this one, all those empty bedrooms, unused bathrooms, a dust-filled attic; ground floor is the kitchen, library, dining rooms, three studies, and Reid's seldom-used home office; and below, in the basement, an extensive garage to house six vehicles, and a high-tech wine cellar, its old wine in old bottles protected by a keypad and code. Valerie's got no interest in booze.

Valerie drops the mail on the pine tabletop and sets about making a fresh pot of coffee. She eyes all the ingredients for the birthday cake, laid out beside the knife block—nothing more she needs to get—then opens the dishwasher that Alek failed to properly close. After restacking the contents, she shuts the door once more with the worn patience of a crucified saint, and returns to the task of coffee.

Alek's a sweet kid, mostly.

Not really a kid, she supposes; he's eighteen but seems younger. Some kids grow up faster when they're neglected, but she guesses it was *only* emotional neglect in Alek's case: that all his other needs were met so that maybe kept him a bit childish, needy. Valerie knew his mother in high school—it wasn't like they were friends, they didn't hang out then or when they had their kids—but she was needy too, Laura Lane that was. Whatever void she thought marriage to Reid 'Red' Howard might fill apparently remained empty and one day when Alek was nine, Laura packed her bags and was gone. Then there was a series of housekeepers and private tutors who didn't last; it wasn't like Alek was especially bad, but his need for attention and reassurance were *constant* and if that wasn't met ... well, Reid had told her that as a kid Alek would make a lot of noise; as a young teen his silence was positively apocalyptic. No one lasted, their nerves shredded one way or another; no one until Valerie.

Alek's father could have sent him to university anywhere, even Ivy League, but had kept him at home to attend the small one with no real reputation in the next town over. There's nothing wrong with it, per se, but not so much to recommend Addison U either (oh, it's got 'University' in its title, but it's really just a college). There's a pretty campus, solid syllabi, decent teachers, no big scandals so far, small class sizes, and a relatively low-level drug problem. Kids who go there do so mainly on one-year transfer programs to Syracuse or Cornell or Princeton. Of course, more than one girl from a disadvantaged background attends there on the Laura Lane-Howard Scholarships Reid set up in the wake of his wife's leaving.

Alek doesn't seem to mind; Reid handed down the black Mercedes C-300 Coupe for him to drive, and he doesn't need to over-extend himself to achieve at Addison. He doesn't really seem to want to go anywhere else.

An easy ride is fine if your life doesn't change, Valerie thinks. But life *does* change, as she knows all too well. It changes when you're not looking, or even when you are looking but you've got your hands full with other stuff. At some point Alek's going to find life kicking his ass to the curb with a vengeance. Deprived of a mother's love, with an absentee father, the kid's so desperate for affection and attention that he applies girls to his ego like they're nicotine patches.

But he's not a bad kid, she thinks, for all that. He's just coping the way he knows how, following a need the only way he thinks he can. She suspects he doesn't like that echo of emptiness most folk experience in their lives; some recognize it, embrace it, some ignore it, flee from it. Some days Valerie thinks she hears the sad chimes of his hollowness dueting with hers, just when she thinks she's got it beat.

She pours a cup of coffee, breathes the aroma deeply as it fills the kitchen in a way that seems too big to come from such a small receptacle. It's magic, she thinks: the smell of it, the ritual of making, the effect it has on the senses. Strange that something so bitter can make you so content. She sits down and sorts the letters into piles. She opens the bills first; they'll get paid with the credit card Reid gave her. She pushes the pink envelope to the corner of the table for Alek to find when he gets home later tonight.

Valerie eyes the pink rectangle, wondering idly about the latest. She's always kind of amazed when the boy looks at her like she's some sort of witch every time she says, 'What's this one's name?' Like he's some great man of mystery. *Lord, sweetheart*, she thinks, *for a smart boy you are dumb.* She could tell him he's predictable, and only the names change. She could tell him she sets her watch by him. But she doesn't.

When she first moved into the Howard Estate, Valerie would sometimes meet the girl for coffee and whatever cake grief required after the inevitable happened: Alek lost interest in the she-of-the-moment. Valerie'd listen to the crying and/or ranting; she'd nod then tell the girl how life was likely to be. There's no great harm in Alek, she'd say, but he's a heedless boy. You don't want a heedless boy; they never notice what you need, or if they do they probably won't give it to you unless they can see an advantage in it for themselves. And heedless boys become heedless men, unless they get taught hard lessons early on.

Not all men, Valerie'd say, but enough of them to make life fucking difficult.

'You make your choice,' she'd tell them. 'Do you want to be the one to teach him those hard lessons? Coz I can tell you now, he'll listen but he'll start thinking of you as his mother, and trust me: no man wants to sleep with his mother. Those that do are not the ones *you* want to sleep with. Or do you want a man who's already had his lessons taught him by someone else?'

She'd never had one of those girls decide she wanted to be the one to teach Alek his lessons, although one did accuse Valerie of being an enabler. When she'd finished laughing, Valerie said 'What's enabling about encouraging a girl to walk away? If I tell you to stay and fight, to bang your head against a wall trying to force someone to love you, what the fuck kind of favor am I doing you? Enabling is sending a battalion of girls back over and over again like cannon fodder because they think they're going to win. You keep going back then what's he going to learn about consequence? Enough women walk away, maybe he'll wake up to himself.'

She'd shaken her head and finished with, 'One day you might have kids and you need to remember that you're the one who teaches your son how much shit a woman will put up with.'

Eventually, though, she got exhausted by the stream of girls and in the end she told Alek to stop bringing them home until he found one he thought he wanted to marry. Really though, she knew somewhere deep down that fighting to force anyone to make better decisions was a lost cause.

Valerie likes to think that her daughter wouldn't have needed that sort of advice. Valerie likes to think her daughter would have been too smart to put up with that kind of juvenile shit. Valerie likes to imagine her life in Mercy's Brook if Lily hadn't gone; although 'likes' probably isn't the right word. It's more like mental cutting. She doesn't pull her own hair, tear at her cuticles, she doesn't drink or smoke or do drugs; no, Valerie's self-harm is imagining better days that'll never ever come.

Lily would have graduated high school, she'd have gone on

to university in New York or Boston. She'd have decided on being a doctor, lawyer, architect: she had all the choices in the world. Maybe she'd have come home to Mercy's Brook, maybe she'd have settled elsewhere and Valerie would have gone to visit. Maybe Chase would have come too; maybe Chase wouldn't have started drinking if their daughter hadn't disappeared. Maybe Valerie wouldn't have started an affair with the man who ran the drugstore. Maybe if they'd had some answers about Lily's fate the other stuff wouldn't have happened.

Or maybe it all would have happened anyway.

Valerie rubs a hand over her face and yawns. She's not sleeping well, the dreams have come in force. They always do around this time. Even if she didn't look at a calendar, she'd still know the date was on the horizon for the physical and psychic effects its forward march caused. It's not helped this year by the sense of helplessness that's crept over her: every avenue seems to have closed down, not a clue left behind as to what happened to Lily.

Sighing, she reaches for the sole envelope with her name on it. She examines again the familiar old-fashioned handwriting, a style learned under threat of a ruler to the knuckles. Valerie's about to slide a long nail under the edge of the flap and begin the delicate process of working it open when the doorbell rings.

Alek lied about the late lecture, and he's surprised he got away with it. Normally Valerie knows his schedule like the back of her hand, but she's been tired lately and when she's tired, she gets distracted. Alek turns left instead of right, heads around the outskirts of Mercy's Brook instead of through the middle so there's less chance of being seen.

Valerie nicknames his various girlfriends after weather

phenomena with a weary boredom. Hurricane Suzie. The French Tempest. Cyclone Elaine. He asks her every time how she knows he's got a new one and she just gives him *the* look, which is part of why he lied about tonight.

As Alek pulls up out front of Carrie's place, the butterflies begin their dance in his tummy. It's a big house, but there are more bodies rolling around inside this one than his: both parents, three sisters, four brothers, and a grandmother. A proper family lives here. A proper family who, according to Carrie, are all out today. The house isn't as big the one he came from—not as much money here as Reid has to throw about—but Carrie's not one of the scholarship students either. She lives ten minutes out of town, twenty minutes from his home, and situated well off the main road, so he doesn't worry about anyone seeing him here. It's early days yet, and one thing he's learning is not to advertise his latest infatuation too soon, and not just because Valerie will make fun of him.

'this is a small town, Alek, it's kind of stuck in time, a very particular time with a set of very particular expectations,' she'd said a few weeks ago at dinner. 'You start seeing a girl, taking her out in public—and sweet Jesus, I am not telling you to sneak around like you're ashamed—but out in front of everyone? Once it's in the open, child, you don't get to enjoy anything in private. Everyone's watching, and every girl with dreams that revolve around a white dress and a charge card she doesn't have to make payments on is looking at you like you're the prized hog at the fair.'

'Hog? Well, as long as it's the prized one ...'

They'd laughed, but then she'd gotten serious again. 'Ask yourself how much you're going to have to apologize for, Alek Howard. Think before you do something dumb, that's all I'm asking.'

Now, he's still sitting in the driver's seat. In his backpack is a box of chocolates, Fair Trade and expensive, the kind Carrie likes; buying them seemed like a good idea at the time, but now … he's not sure about taking them in. Is it too much or too little or should he just turn up empty-handed and see what happens?

It's only been a week, jeez. He used to think he was being generous—if his father had taught him nothing else it was generosity—but Alek's wondering if it sends the wrong signal. *Creates too many expectations, too soon*. Valerie's voice is in his head nowadays. Shit, he can't even give a girl a box of chocolates without second-guessing himself.

How much are you going to have to apologize for?

The front door to the house opens and there's Carrie hanging in the doorway, all that long dark hair, wide dark eyes, slow smile and tanned skin.

Alek grabs the backpack. He'll see how things pan out.

'Mornin', Valerie.'

Sheriff Obadiah Tully is a barrel on short, skinny legs. His uniforms are specially made, but even personalized tailoring isn't a silver bullet, not with his eccentricities of form. Valerie thinks it unfair that Tully shouldn't have to worry about being beach-body ready; she'd love for him to be afflicted with just a small degree of the self-doubt that comes with being female. But nope, he just hitches his utility belt where it hangs under the awning of his gut with a peacock flourish.

'Sheriff. What brings you to my door?'

'Well, not exactly *your* door is it, Valerie?' Tully's never quite got over his pique at that.

As Tully's investigation into Lily's disappearance went nowhere, Valerie's complaints got louder and louder, while her husband got drunker and drunker. Obadiah took it upon himself to sometimes tail her when she drove home late at night, or follow her up and down the aisles at the supermarket, making sure she knew he was there. He'd convinced both the State Police and the FBI that Lily Wynne had run away from home; under his telling, the honors student became a hellion with a turning of the tongue.

Then Chase Wynne emptied their bank accounts and left Mercy's Brook.

Then the bookstore where Valerie worked closed and she was out of a job.

Then the house had to be sold and things looked pretty grim.

That was when Reid Howard stepped in—almost a year to the day after Lily's vanishing—and offered her a job and a home and a child, of sorts. Tully wasn't brave enough to keep tormenting her after that, so it made Valerie wonder just what the hell Shitheel Tully was doing here now.

'Is there something I can help you with, Obadiah? Or are you just here to exchange pleasantries?'

'I just thought you might like to know that Lucius Anderson passed.'

'Passed what? Wind? *Passed*: that is the stupidest term I've ever heard.' Valerie's blowing smoke to cover the effect of the news, but unease and not a little sadness are making her stomach churn. She swallows, thinking of the last time she spoke with Lucius—well, argued with him. She thinks of the envelope on the kitchen table, the distinctive handwriting. 'What happened?'

'Home invasion,' says Tully. He pushed the hat back on his forehead, showing the receding grey hairline and the indentations where the band is too tight.

'Home invasion? Around here?' Her disbelief is clear, and it's not like the Sheriff should expect anything else, but still he draws himself up, a bantam rooster puffing his chest like he's about to do battle.

'You know there are meth labs back in the woods. There are folk passing through our little town who're happy to do ill. You should know that better than anyone, Valerie Wynne.'

'What would some meth-chef want in Lucius Anderson's *home*? He didn't keep anything there, not when he had an entire drugstore filled with medicines.'

'Well, maybe some *meth-chef* wouldn't know that?'

'Isn't it something you should be figuring out?'

'You know, I'm only here as a kindness, seeing as how he meant something to you. Or maybe he didn't.'

'Whatever passed between me and Lucius is none of your business.' Valerie's hand on the doorframe is shaking, and she can feel cold sweat breaking out under her arms, down in the small of her back. She clears her throat, thinks of the letter inside again. 'Look. I'm sorry, Obadiah, I don't want to pick a fight with you. I'm just ... shocked. I'm shocked, is all.'

He shuffles back a few steps as if surprised by her conciliation, then nods. He narrows his eyes and asks in an offhanded manner, 'You hadn't spoken to him recently? Lucius? He didn't mention anything to you?'

And Valerie sees where this has been leading. 'Like if he was afraid of anyone? Or he'd seen someone hanging around outside at odd hours? Like that?'

'Yeah, like that.'

She shakes her head. 'Obadiah, you know things didn't end well between me and Lucius.' And truly they had not for he'd thought she would fall into a marriage with him after Chase left. 'I'm the last person he'd confide in.' But she thinks of seeing him in the supermarket last week, how he looked like he wanted to say something but then turned away. She shrugs, makes a peace offering of her hand, which Tully takes in surprise. She hopes she hasn't laid it on too thick. 'Will you keep me informed? I did care for him, no matter what happened.'

She closes the door before he's at his car. She doesn't hear if the engine starts or not, if he leaves the estate. She's got other things on her mind.

Valerie'd never thought Tully had anything to do with Lily's disappearance; she'd never thought he might be covering up for someone; she just thought him incompetent and spiteful, and she'd never kept that opinion to herself. Now, she leans against the door, feels the wood solid at her back as a wave of nausea washes over her.

In her dreams, Lily calls for her, Lily in her black, sequined prom dress and the pretty red high-heels, Lily with her dark hair swept up in a stylish chignon because the girl always had her very own tastes. Lily who disappeared the day before her prom on her way home from the shoe store on Main Street where she'd gone to get those gel pads to stop her feet slipping out of those red silk shoes.

In reality, Lily'd never got a chance to wear that dress or shoes for real, so the memory Valerie has is of the test run at home when she and Lily experimented with makeup and hair. When Lily perfected her stride in those high heels, pacing along the hallway upstairs until she got the sway just right.

But still, that's the Lily who haunts Valerie's dreams, although sometimes it's Valerie's own face she sees in place of her daughter's.

Back in the kitchen Valerie sits at the table before her knees give way. In front of her are the now-cold coffee and that envelope. Lucius Anderson had told her one afternoon as they lay side by side, naked and sweat-covered, that he'd been taught penmanship by his strict grandfather, that other kids laughed at him because no one else made their letters just-so.

Valerie thinks Lucius must have mailed the letter just before he was killed. She wonders if Obadiah Tully suspected something of the sort. She tears open the envelope, slides the single white sheet of paper out and unfolds it.

In the same elaborate handwriting are the words 'Security camera, Anderson's Drugstore', then: 'I'm sorry'. That's all, just those words in the middle of the page and she draws a blank as to the meaning. Then her brain kicks along and she turns the thing over; the breath falls out of her.

In black and white print, ink jet because her sweating fingers smudge the edge of the image: there's a familiar black Mercedes C300 Coupe heading down Main Street. The date stamp is the same day Lily Wynne disappeared, and the time shows a good hour after everything closed and the strip was deserted because folk had homes to get to and meals to prepare.

And Valerie leans closer and closer because the photo's been taken on an angle that means she can see straight through the windscreen, can see clearly the driver's head and the passenger's.

It *could* mean nothing, she tells herself, and that car might not have had anything to do with Lily's disappearance. It *would* mean nothing, she tells herself, if she didn't know the car and driver all too well. If it wasn't Lily in the passenger seat, laughing. Valerie throws up all over the kitchen table.

John Wick is on the screen, deadpanning his way through a myriad of killings. Carrie's in Alek's lap, their soundtrack is a series of gunshots, of the gasps of dying men until from elsewhere in the house there's the sound of a door closing, then voices, a female and children. He's very gentle as he moves Carrie onto the sofa next to him, then shuffles a few inches to his left, adjusting himself slightly. On the coffee table is a half-empty box of chocolates, the kind she likes, that Carrie'd presented him as a birthday present.

Carrie pouts, but laughs, reaches for another chocolate. She smells like vanilla. It's nice. *This is nice*, thinks Alek.

'Don't worry: Mom will be supervising homework for a while yet.' The girl settles into the corner of the sofa, kneads her toes against his thigh. 'Hey, when did your dad get back?'

'He's not home.'

'No,' she says. 'I saw him this morning.'

'You must have made a mistake.' Alek sits up straighter.

'I was out jogging on the Mason Road, he slowed down and waved at me.' She purses her lips. 'You know, I do *know* your dad when I see him.'

Carrie smiles around her snippy tone, and Alek feels a tingling down his spine, not fast, but creeping, like there's a spider with eight cold feet trying not to be noticed.

Reid had paid attention to Alek's girlfriends in the past and some he'd taken as easily as picking an apple. He didn't do it for a relationship—none of them lasted longer than a single night, dinner and bed—Reid did it because he could. Alek thought about Annie and Ellie, Elaine and Sukie, scholarship girls he'd met at Addison U. All smart and ambitious, but disadvantaged in one way or another, orphans or fostered, poor, from the small towns in the more remote parts of the state. The towns that had boomed in the early days but through which even the Greyhounds now roared without stopping.

Sometimes his father was one of the reasons Alek didn't stick with a girl, but he'd never told Valerie *that* because how pathetic was it? Having your dad steal your girlfriends? Besides, Valerie and Reid, they'd been friends at school, and if Alek told Valerie something that made her not want to hang around any longer, then where would he be? It's not just the threat of having to feed himself, it's the idea of no voice but his own, no face but his own in that big house. Valerie had made him feel not so alone; she saw something in him that was worthwhile, and he saw himself reflected better in her than the hallway mirrors.

His mobile vibrates in his pocket, and he plucks it out to read the text.

'I better go,' he says to Carrie's surprised displeasure. Alek has to admit his interest in her has lessened in a very short space of time. He'd seen the look on Carrie's face when she mentioned his father, noticed the way she'd blushed and smiled, was flattered at unwarranted attention from a gray fox, and a rich gray fox at that.

'Why?' Carrie pouts.

'Valerie needs me at home.'

'Well.' And her mouth twists, turns sour where it had been so sweet and full mere minutes ago. 'Wouldn't want to let Valerie down.'

'No,' he says, rising. And because it's the truth, he doesn't blush or feel ashamed. 'I wouldn't.'

New wine in old bottles ...

The keypad is blinking slowly at her, an arrogant stare. She doesn't know the code. Six digits. If she inputs the wrong numbers, what happens? An alarm goes off somewhere? The private security firm will call the house and she'll answer, tell them it was an accident. Still and all, better no one knows she's snooping.

At first she'd thought about the garage—it was only natural, given sight of the Mercedes—but she'd been in there before. She's been in all the rooms of the house, it held no secrets for her. Except for one spot; one spot she'd had no interest in. *This one room.*

She puts her face against the dull silver of the door, feels it cool as death on her skin, sees her own reflection as a strange blurred shadow. Valerie presses her ear to the metal and listens as hard as she can, although she's not sure what she might hear. Whether it's with hope or fear, she doesn't know, but she still does it.

Nothing. There's nothing.

Valerie thinks about how she's never questioned this room's purpose. She thinks about how smart he was as he gave her the tour of the house the day she moved in. She recalls him walking her down the stairs to the basement, and along the stone corridor; he'd made sure they stopped outside the door, pointed it out. He'd even poked a finger at the keypad like an uncoordinated child, making *beep-boop* noises. He smiled.

'Wine cellar. It's very high-tech for all the investment bottles. Not your vino. No new wine in these old bottles,' he'd said and laughed—Valerie remembered in school him telling it like an old joke, explaining that his own father had used it to refer to children. Explaining it hadn't made it any funnier. 'I can give you the code, if you like? Do you want to have a look?'

She'd shaken her head. Valerie had no interest in booze, not given Chase's drinking habits, and Reid Howard had known that.

'Not even a little curious? Don't even want a peek?' he teased. They'd laughed, then moved on.

'I don't drink, Reid,' she'd reminded him and seen that strange satisfaction on his face.

'Sorry. I forgot about Chase.' Even though there'd been an element of *sorry, not sorry* about it, she'd shrugged it off; the room made no impression on her memory. There's a fully stocked bar upstairs, more wine and spirits than anyone, including a teenage boy and his friends, could get through. No need for Alek to come down here. The cellar was out of sight, out of mind for both of them.

Valerie pushes away from the door and looks at the green lights flashing in their usual sequence again.

Six numbers.

New wine in old bottles.

She puts her hand out, almost touches the keypad. She hesitates, her fingertips hovering so close, so close. What if she's wrong?

What would happen?

But if she didn't try. If she waited until he came home, she'd never be able to hide what she suspected. If she didn't find out now she might not be able to control herself when he finally returned.

Valerie touches the numbers that make up Alek's birthday.

The keypad blinks angry red at her, makes a low, flat sound of disapproval. Too much to hope for, she supposes. Too easy. Her hands shake, her fingers go cold with disappointment. Then ... then it occurs that there's one more number she might try.

Valerie picks out the numbers of tomorrow's date, the anniversary of Lily's disappearance.

The seconds after the last number are the longest she's ever lived. The keypad beeps, the lock clicks. Valerie pushes the silver door open and steps through.

No blood, no bones bleached by either sun or moon.

What did she expect?

Not this.

It's a huge room, white-painted and filled with ... shelves and pedestals.

There's a short flight of stainless steel stairs that take her from the landing just inside the door down to the floor of the cellar. Valerie steps up to the first pedestal: it's waist-high and made of thick green glass. And on it, just like on all the other pedestals and shelves, is a pair of pretty, high-heeled shoes. All around, shoes for a variety of special occasions. She leans forward, looks more closely at the nearest ones: pink shoes, prom shoes, diamantes on the straps, as well as specks of dried blood.

Valerie moves on to the next display: black stilettos, red Louboutin soles, dull brown splotches adhering to the ebony leather.

Next: purple patent, no designer label, cheap and nasty and stained.

A pair of light green Jimmy Choos.

All the colors of the rainbow, all styles, from all manner of economic strata and different fashion eras.

It's a while before she finds Lily's.

It takes all of her self-control not to rush around, making increasingly high-pitched noises, desperately seeking the red silk shoes. She knows if she lets herself do that she'd lose all semblance of control; she'd just sit on the floor rocking and weeping, and she'd stay there until Doomsday.

She's so intent on concentrating on *just the next pair* that she's stunned to discover them in front of her. Lily's lovely prom shoes. In patches, the red silk is darker where blood has soaked in.

And that is all her daughter has been reduced to: this pair of ruined footwear. There's nothing else in the whole place, no other doors or rooms, no hint as to where the rest of her child might be.

Just the shoes.

How many pairs? A hundred, perhaps?

No bodies.

Just the shoes.

Row upon row.

Valerie reaches out. These are all she's got, probably all she'll ever have of her baby ever again. They are surprisingly sturdy, the stiletto heels tough, no matter how delicate they look.

'Don't touch.' The tone is sharp, so commanding that Valerie hesitates, is almost tempted to obey. 'It's a rare collection, as I told you before, Valerie.'

'Fuck you,' she says and wraps a hand around the right shoe. She curls it into her chest, cradling it. Then she turns to face him.

Reid Howard is handsome though not especially tall—a head shorter than Valerie, not much difference between him and Obadiah Tully, frankly—and dressed far more casually than his usual tailored business suit: dark jeans, t-shirt, Timberlands. Alek's got his features but not his red hair. Reid doesn't have a beard, he's clean-shaven, and his eyes are a clear green. He's as popular with women as his son is—God knows Valerie almost fell for it herself once before coming to her senses—he's got no reason to hurt girls, but Valerie guesses he just likes it.

But she senses she needs more time, she needs to stall, so she asks, 'Why? Why would you take her? You barely knew her, she was nothing to you. Why take her? Why take my child then bring me to look after *yours*?'

His grin as he walks down the steps, heavy boots punctuating the silence, tells her *Because I could*. The smile slips between her ribs, lodges like a knife in her heart. 'I do like you, Valerie, never doubt that. But your baby looked just like you did in high school, just like when you said *no* to me, and *yes* to that idiot, Chase. Then Lucius—fucking Lucius! I'm a patient man, but I'm not very forgiving.' His smile widens. 'And why wouldn't Lily accept a lift home from her momma's old friend?' He shrugs. 'You being here kept you under my eye, stopped fricking Tully complaining about you—Lord you have irritated him over the years. The bonus was you looked after my idiot son. He behaves himself, I'm not distracted from either business or pleasure.' He raises his hands, palms up. 'I took one child away, but I gave you another. You're very fond of Alek. In a way, it all evens out, yes?'

It takes a moment before shock wrings a shriek of 'No!'

from Valerie; her fingers tighten convulsively on the shoe.

'No?' He feigns surprise. 'Ah well. How did you get in?'

'New wine in old bottles. At first I thought it was Alek, but you meant *my* new wine.' Part of her mind is astonished to be having this conversation so coolly. But she's got to keep a clear head, if she wants to survive. Reid's produced a knife, the biggest from the block in the kitchen, which he taps against the glass of the shelves and pedestals as he passes, the sound a strange singing.

'Ah.' He smiles wryly. 'I shouldn't have underestimated you. Too clever by half, you, too clever to get into my bed. Still, everyone makes mistakes: not too clever to marry Chase or fuck Anderson though.'

'Lucius? Did you ... ?'

'Tully said he was wavering. You'd pissed him off by leaving—you do piss men off, Valerie, it is one of your defining traits—and I'd bailed him out, he was hemorrhaging money on some bad investments, so it was as much venal as vengeful. Oh, he didn't know what had happened to your Lily—don't think that of him. He believed I'd dropped her on the way home and she'd met her fate elsewhere, but his conscience was starting to get to him, and he was starting to wonder why it needed to be kept from you. When he was angry at you he was happy to play along.'

'Everyone makes mistakes,' she can't help but say. He snorts.

'Should have chosen me, Valerie, or at least for a little while.'

'Why are you home? Now?' He never bothered to come home for his son's birthday, but ...

'The anniversary, Valerie. I love watching you every year on the day Lily disappeared. You're strangely radiant with grief, it's quite bewitching. I wouldn't miss that for the world.'

Valerie begins backing away as he comes closer. 'What

about Alek?'

'What about him? I'll tell him you left. I'll tell him you got tired of him, just like his mother did, that you were disappointed in him. He's used to that. He won't pursue it. Kid never sticks at anything, you know that better than anyone.'

'He's not like he was. You wouldn't know, you're never home. You don't know your own son.' A burst of hysterical laughter catches in her throat at the morbid domesticity of the argument, two parents in a tug-of-war over a child. 'He's not the boy you made anymore; he's not *your* new wine.'

'Granted you've helped him settle down, it keeps him out of trouble, but even if you hadn't made this ill-considered incursion into my space your time was coming to an end. I worry he'll develop too much of a conscience if you're around much longer and that's an inconvenient thing. Best you be gone, let him think himself deserted once again.' He tilts his head, pondering. 'Do you think you're so fierce about protecting him because you failed Lily?'

She swallows, doesn't answer that, instead says, 'Where …'

'What?'

'Where's his mother?'

Reid points to the far end of the cellar; Valerie can make out a worn pair of white sandals with wedge heels. Long out of fashion.

'Laura didn't go willingly. She did love her boy.'

'Dad?'

Both of them whirl to find Alek on the landing at the entrance to the cellar, in answer to Valerie's text to come home, sent because she couldn't think of anyone else she needed by her. His hands are held up in a gesture of surrender. Behind him, Obadiah Tully stands, his service weapon pointed at the boy's back.

· · ·

Alek is slow as he takes the stairs, not just because of the gun barrel that periodically pokes him in the ribs. He's heard everything Reid and Valerie had to say, and seen his own reflection in the steel of the door, as if his father's words have remade him into something shadowy. Destabilized. His stare moves from his father to his tutor, to the shelves and shoes, the ceiling, the floor, the walls. He's still processing everything he heard before Tully appeared and gestured for him to enter the cellar.

Tully's footsteps have stopped, but Alek keeps going for some paces. He looks over his shoulder at the Sheriff. Tully's face is a picture. He's clearly never been down here, just like Alek, only his expression is one of realizing just how deep a hole he's stepped into. Alek guesses Obadiah's been happy enough to take Reid's money to smooth things over, inconvenient investigations and the like, but he didn't really appreciate what Reid was doing. Alek had no idea himself and now he wonders on which side of the line Tully will fall.

He stops by a pedestal, takes in the cheap purple patents; they're eye-catching, not something he's likely to forget even with no particular interest in footwear. His head tilts to the side and he reaches out to touch them. 'Annie's.' His gaze moves on, he points at a pair of knock-off Prada pumps in electric blue. 'Ellie's.'

Somewhere in the cellar, Alek thinks, Elaine and Sukie's shoes also await. All the Howard Scholarship girls, the girls Alek didn't see again. He didn't bother with them after they'd seen his father, he'd wiped them away to salve his hurt boy's pride. Abandoned them. He tries to swallow but it's hard, like there's a rock in his throat.

'Dad,' he says again, noting the kitchen knife Reid's carrying. Alek feels sick. Sick and sad and pained. He says it again, as if it's the only thought that's in his brain. 'Dad.'

'Alek. Terrible timing, my boy, as always.' Reid shakes his head.

'What you gonna do with them, Reid?' When Tully's voice comes, it's clear he's made his choice; any hopes Alek had that the Sheriff might have chosen to help are swiftly gone. In the hole, Obadiah's going to keep digging. Holes, Alek wants to remind him, don't work like that.

'Well, my lovely Valerie here is going to meet with an accident—you don't need to be here for that and probably best if he isn't either. Obadiah, take Alek to the kitchen and sit with him until I'm done.'

'You can't be serious, Reid. Kid's not going to keep his mouth shut.'

'He's my son and he'll do what I tell him to.' Reid raises his knife, not in threat but more as a lecturer would a pointer or a cane: *Attend to this, Tully, if you know what's good for you.*

Alek, standing between his father and the Sheriff, notices what the grown men have forgotten: Valerie. Reid's got his back to her, Tully's attention is on Reid with the sort of tunnel vision that's rendered him one of the worst investigators Mercy's Brook has ever had the misfortune to employ. But Alek can see her from the corner of his eye—clear as a perfect reflection—and he's careful not to draw their gaze to her as she inches closer to Reid. Her footsteps are light, so light, but still there's a whisper of her approach and his father seems set to turn.

Alek repeats, 'Dad?'

Reid looks at him with irritation as Valerie unfurls the hand from her chest and raises the red shoe. Alek sees her rush forward, and he pivots, drops his shoulder and charges at Tully, who doesn't even get a shot off, but tips straight back, his head striking the rise of the bottom steps. Obadiah's eyes stay open, his stare uncomprehending.

Alek sits up, rubbing his shoulder. He hears the noise his

father makes but it takes him a few moments to gather himself and look.

Valerie stands over Reid Howard, who's on his knees, swaying, a red stiletto heel buried in the top of his head. He looks as surprised as Tully, although more outraged. Then he loses his grip on life and gravity takes over, slowly he flops face-forward onto the polished concrete.

As far as Mercy's Brook is concerned, Obadiah Tully died a hero, saving Valerie and Alek from Reid Howard's psychotic episode, before his own untimely demise. No bodies have been found in the grounds of the estate, and the Mayor is happy with that since he considers a graveyard of girls might be bad for the town's morale and future economic prospects. *Least said, soonest mended and all that,* he says to Valerie and Alek, meaning *Keep your mouths shut and no one looks at your actions too closely.* The hastily-appointed new Sheriff keeps telling Valerie that they might never find anything more than the shoe collection.

Valerie keeps the red stilettos in a box in her cupboard. If she could, she would get rid of the memory of that day, but it's like a golden key with blood on it that she can't rub off. Some nights she re-dreams the moment in the cellar with its collection of pretty, bloody shoes; she dreams Alek is much smaller, younger, that he says 'Daddy', and Reid takes the boy's hand in a way he never did in life.

Some nights, too, she dreams that he turns into his father. She dreams that the apple hasn't fallen that far from the tree, that he might have no choice in any of it, that the switch will flick whether either of them wants it to or not. But she also knows he made his choice about who he wanted to be.

Lily doesn't come to her in dreams anymore, though, and she can't quite work out if it's a gift or a curse.

WILDERLING

The kid appeared on the first of May.

LP was in the kitchen, doing the dishes in desultory fashion, cursing Kurt's refusal to shell out for a dishwasher ('Already got one and she cooks too,' accompanied by a slap on the ass was his standard reply), and staring at the overgrown foliage of the back yard; it tangled with the old growth woods their property bordered. It was the movement that caught her eye, slow but still kinda sharp, cautious and nervous, and pretty soon there was this kid creeping out of the trees and shrubs and long grass.

Matted dark hair, halfway down the back, no clothes to speak of but so covered in filth that LP couldn't tell if it was a girl or a boy. Lordy, but it must reek to high heaven. She wondered if the kid could see her, but realized its gaze wasn't directed at her, or the windows she stood behind, but at the fat tortoiseshell tom.

It was Tuesday, and quiet. LP's best friend Angie had been sick, so she'd not dropped Thomas off for his once-a-week day with 'Aunty'; he was a good baby, contented, seldom cried, but she was always aware of his presence. Kurt was long since gone to work at the furniture factory. The houses on either side were empty and had been for some time, with foreclosure signs decorating their front yards like great steaming turds. LP was deeply grateful for the respite as the Mondays she spent with her mother were invariably hellish, and yesterday had been a high-water mark.

Whiskey was sunning himself on the little round iron table that had been quietly rusting in the garden for ten years. It sat just off to one side of the washing line, didn't get in the way, could barely hold the weight of a cat or a peg-basket. There were two chairs to go with it, but no one sat on them anymore on account of the legs being held together with what passed for oxidized spit, and the tendrils of some mysterious weed that wound its way through the lacework.

LP told herself she couldn't have done anything, couldn't have changed what happened, but she was lying and she knew it. Sure, she wouldn't have made it to the back door and into the yard, but she could have banged on the glass. Kurt loved that damned cat more than life itself, and maybe more than her, but it jumped and hissed if *she* so much as breathed near it; anything louder would have made the critter shit itself and run. But she didn't trouble to make a noise, in fact she held her breath, just waiting to see what might happen. She rubbed one damp hand absently across the flat belly beneath her cotton dress, primped the short dark curls of her ghostly reflection with the other.

Whiskey didn't even see it coming.

Which meant the kid was *silent*, like stealthy as a fox, light as a breeze, because the kid's fingers—closer up now, LP could see how long the nails were, black ragged things—were around Whiskey's thick neck before he knew it. That neck was broken in a freakishly swift motion—there was no doubt the cat was dead, the way it hung in that strong, nasty little grip.

But LP couldn't muster even a lick of sympathy for the

feline. Too many years of him tearing up her favorite cushions and couches, her craft supplies and works-in-progress, her clothes whenever he could get his paws on them, and the smell of piss in the house because Kurt wouldn't get the fucking animal neutered. There were deep red scratches on her arms, the latest in a series of Whiskey's 'love taps' while she slept; she'd got infections from them three times before. LP felt the first genuine smile in a long while lift her lips, and imagining life without Whiskey distracted her from watching the kid tear him open and feast on his innards. She kind of glanced off to the side, so she saw but not *quite*.

When the cat was no more than a sack of bloodied fur and bones, the wilderling tossed Whiskey on top of the little iron table again, almost well-mannered, and disappeared back into the woods. LP would go out soon and put him in the compost, bury him deep in the rotting food scraps and other crap in the plastic bin that sometimes swelled in the summer heat and always smelled bad, so bad even Whiskey never went near it. Kurt wouldn't look for his old tom there.

LP went back to doing the dishes, humming, heart considerably lighter.

'Angie, you ever hear of kids lost in the woods hereabouts? Not ever coming out again?'

LP had spent part of a day at the library, using their internet so Kurt couldn't check up on her browsing history at home. He didn't do it to keep track of her or anything—he wasn't that kind of husband—but he liked to find reasons to tease her and LP was an inveterate adopter of hobbies. She always began with online research. Kurt thought he was being funny, didn't notice her gritted teeth.

So she'd sat in the air-conditioning, ignoring the low-level buzz of people and machines, and looked through old news articles for mention of children who'd disappeared from their homes or schools or the national forest ... anywhere, really. But there was just the usual: parents kidnapping their own offspring in custody disputes; random crimes of opportunity by would-be killers and/or pedophiles—those children were always returned in one state or another, some less alive than others, some wishing they'd not survived. Then there were the ones who just wandered in the front door later than usual, had lost track of time, or tried to run away from but decided that, somehow, home was safer than the big old world.

In fact, it appeared, from LP's reading, that Wolf's Briar held an unusual record, that of a one hundred percent return of its roaming children (dead or alive, but always returned). So, she'd called Angie, because any bit of gossip Angie didn't know wasn't worth having, especially seeing as how she worked for the local police department. Not that she had loose lips, hell no—Angie wouldn't have kept her job if Sheriff Bagley thought she was leaking secrets like a sieve—but, as she'd said to LP, she needed someone to vent to on occasion. All those notions, all those bits of truth, all those terrible things, pressed inside her so much that sometimes she thought her skin would split. So she told LP and she knew LP could be trusted because they'd been best friends since grade school; not to mention that LP had no one else she'd call 'close', so who was she gonna tell? Not that Angie would ever have said that aloud, but LP knew she knew, and appreciated her friend's discretion.

Given her research results, LP thought she probably already knew the answer to her question, but she'd asked anyway. Just to be sure.

'You mean proper dead?' Angie was at work, so her voice was low. LP could imagine her friend's blue eyes skirting the office to make sure no one was within hearing range, her shoulders a little hunched, pen tapping on the blotter on her desk. For someone who kept secrets so well, Angie sure had a lot of tells; she'd have made a crappy poker player.

'Nope. Missing, never found again. Maybe ten years ago?'

She hadn't seen the kid again, not in the last two days since she'd buried Whiskey deep as she could bear in the stinking compost bin. But she felt the kid would be back; she couldn't say how she knew, but sometimes she got feelings, did LP.

'Why are you asking?' Angie said, but LP could hear the tapping of keys as her friend began searching whatever databases police forces were heir to: something sure as shit better than Google at the library. All things considered Angie coped pretty good with the stuff she heard and saw, stuff that had made grown men cry. Pretty damned good, especially since Thomas was only six months old; sure sometimes Angie got distressed, but it didn't seem to make her scared, not for her own kid. She told LP it made her more determined that what she did was important, even if she was only answering the phone and filing and researching. It's *a little bit*, she'd say, *but* it's my *little bit*. She said again, 'Why are you asking?'

LP was careful not to swallow—if Angie was ignorant of her own tells, she knew LP's, and that gulping noise was a dead giveaway—offering casually, 'I thought, you know, I might try writing a story.'

Without children or a job, there wasn't a lot taking up LP's time when Kurt wasn't home from work, so she picked up hobbies the way some men picked up hookers. She'd made dollhouses and miniature furniture for over two years before she got bored; knitted so many sweaters that the Good Will store still had some on their shelves; crocheted blankets, some of which were still in use in the police cells because they were warmer than the cheap rubbish usually purchased; she'd tried painting, jewellery-making, pottery and ceramics (there was a difference), car detailing, landscape gardening, cushion-making, sewing clothes for babies, children, adults and dolls, she'd decorated cakes, done quilting, book-binding, repairing watches, furniture restoration ... You name it, there was a good chance LP had tried it, and when she mastered it, she got bored and cast about for something new—much to Kurt's amusement. So, she didn't think that Angie's radar would ping at something that sounded like another hobby-in-progress.

She was right.

'Well, why not?' said Angie more to herself than LP. Having no craft skills herself, she was always interested in her friend's undertakings. More tapping, some tongue-clicking. 'You know, it does not look like it. Not in that time period. You want me to widen the search parameters? Like, five years either side?'

'Sure, that'd be great.' LP didn't think that would matter, the kid hadn't looked more than ten. Then again, that strength in those hands ... the dirt obscuring mostly everything ...

'So, what's this story about?' Angie was clearly warming to the idea of her friend as a writer.

'Well, I can't tell you yet!' LP said it almost too loud. 'Don't want to jinx myself. Who knows if I can even get the idea on the page. And don't you go telling anyone—last thing I need is Kurt making fun of me for this too.' She sighed. 'This is just for me, something I can keep quiet.'

'My lips are sealed, as you very well know. But promise I can read it when you're done, even if you think it's awful?'

'Okay, promise.'

'Hey, look this search is going slow. I'll call you back if I get any hits?'

'Sure thing. We good for next Tuesday?' Every week they caught up for a cheap movie and drinks at the tiny Royale Cinema, whether there was a new film showing or not.

'Hells yeah. I'll bring Thomas over early in the morning

for his 'aunty day'. Then pick you both up after work, and we can drop him off with Byron on the way to the movies.'

'Sure thing.' LP cared for Thomas because she loved Angie, who'd married Byron straight out of high school and fallen pregnant almost immediately. But she'd lost that baby and the one that came after, and the one after that. So, for a while, it didn't matter that LP (marrying Kurt around the same time), didn't have children either. Didn't matter that she didn't fall no matter how often they did it, in how many positions, with however many potions or pills or injections. Didn't matter because Angie's babies never came to fruition. Not until Thomas. He really wasn't any trouble, slept most of the time he was at LP's, and one day a week was manageable; the bitterness didn't choke her too much, wasn't a constant reminder of opportunities not given to *her*.

Angie's voice sped up, abruptly urgent and running everything together, 'Gottagosheriffscomingbye.'

'Bye,' said LP to dead air.

LP found the fattest, oldest cat she could at one of the Wolf's Briar shelters. Told the woman in charge about Whiskey, how he'd gone missing, how her husband loved that cat so much. And sure, it was a little soon to go replacing dear old Whiskey, but hey, it had to happen sometime and it was awful to have a feline-shaped hole in their lives. The woman nodded sympathetically and asked if she wouldn't rather a younger animal, one that would be with them longer? LP kept her face straight and said she'd rather give a "senior citizen" a great home for however short a time it had left, and the woman wiped away a tear.

LP tied the cat to the iron table, a strand of twine from its collar to the latticework; left it a bowl of milk, some dry food, and the thing seemed happy enough, went to sleep almost immediately. By late afternoon, she wasn't quite so sure that she'd see the wilderling again at all. But about twenty minutes before Kurt was due to walk in the door—and thank God, coz she couldn't bear to present him with another cat to take precedence over her—there was that same slow-quick movement between the trees and soon enough the kid was stepping furtively into the garden, pert little nose twitch-sniffing at whatever odor the old cat was giving off.

The nameless critter went the way of Whiskey; kid ate fast, must have been hungry. LP wondered if it had hunted out its patch of the woods, if the squirrels and raccoons, and whatever else might count as small game had got too wary or too scarce. Or maybe finding Whiskey had just been so easy and the kid had decided it liked *easy*.

From the kitchen window LP watched everything, didn't look away. Maybe coz she had no connection to this animal, or just maybe because she was getting more and more curious. At any rate, she was looking straight at the kid while it licked red off its palms, when it glanced up, straight at where LP stood. This time, LP was sure she'd been *seen*. She held her breath, unmoving. The kid stilled, tilted its head and stared.

LP's curiosity was what got her through boredom, what made her chase hobby after hobby, what stopped her from doing terrible things like taking a hammer to Kurt's big old head at her most frustrated, or pulling a blade across her mother's throat every time Agnes told her what a failure she was. All manner of violent things that occurred to her when someone insulted her or underestimated her and wasn't polite enough to bother to cover it up.

But right *now*? The curiosity that had stirred those few days ago, had kept her looking out for the kid, turn cold as a stone in a mountain stream. Because the kid looked at her as if she was food.

LP had had this vision, of the kid, the kid somehow

becoming *hers*. In her imagination, it was a girl, all clean and neat, in a pretty dress or jeans with flowers embroidered on the hems, hair brushed and shiny, well-mannered and sweet and *tame*. And she thought how if she had that kid, a kid, her kid, then no one would be looking judgment on her ever again. No more pitying stares, no more mouthing of *childless* behind her back when they didn't know she could see them in the reflections in the shop windows or the glass freezer cabinet doors at the supermarket. If she just had that kid ...

Everyone liked Kurt; people liked LP too, but they pitied her, whispered *What a shame, what a shame*, and she knew it. No babies, no children.

It had settled in her, this idea, and although it was shaken somewhat by the kid's feral gaze, it was still there. That's how ideas are, once they take root they've got those little tendrils and if they connect with something you really, really want? Well, then. No matter how bad an idea, it was probably going to stay with you until you got what you wished for, and consequences be damned.

One thing was for sure, LP was gonna need more cats.

After the third cat (sourced from the last of Wolf Briar's shelters), LP set up a little nest in the basement—there was a small space she'd used a couple of years ago as a dark room when photography had occupied her mind. She replaced the lock and made sure it was sturdy. Kurt never went down there, didn't spend time in the shed either, no tinkering for him, just wasn't that kind of guy. Work was work, he'd say, and I wanna leave it *there*. He was a porch-sitter, Kurt was. Come home, get himself a beer from the fridge, kiss her on the forehead, then out to the front of the house and the old swing that creaked and creaked and creaked. He wasn't a bad guy, but she'd got earplugs so she could make dinner without feeling the urge to go out and hit him over the head with a skillet or whatever came to hand. *Earplugs Saved My Marriage!* Some days she thought about writing that story and sending it to one of those magazines, but she figured it was probably a pretty common solution for a lot of women, so she wouldn't be adding anything.

There was a small chest of drawers and a day bed that she cleaned up; its mattress was soft if not a little soggy, but she couldn't imagine the kid had been sleeping on anything especially luxurious—and the tiny room was neat and blacked-out window down there was small, small, small so she didn't believe anyone could crawl out even if they did manage to break the glass. It would just give LP time to get the kid used to her, soon she'd have it taking food from her hand, then ... civilization would ensue. Could the kid talk? LP had no idea.

Kurt had always wanted children, but he'd never made her feel bad about not having them. He had asked if they should go and get tested, figure who wasn't working properly, but LP decided she didn't want to know *that*. Folks automatically blamed her anyway—what if she found out they were right? She preferred it this way. Now, though, there was this kid, a kid, her kid. Their kid. When people asked, LP would say it was a foster. Had a bad start. And Kurt? How was she going to tell Kurt? Honestly, she had no idea, it was a mere detail, but all she could see was the goal, shimmering just out of reach, so she'd burn that bridge when she came to it.

When Monday rolled around the usual pressure had built in her chest, but LP still got out of bed, made peach cobbler while Kurt ate his breakfast. When he was gone, she dragged on a blue dress, sandals with heels and did her hair. The makeup she wore was light, but it wouldn't have mattered if she'd applied it with a trowel; her mother would criticize it either way. Too little and she wasn't trying, too much and she looked like a whore. LP was an only child, but she never wished harder for a sibling than as an adult, just to have someone else to share the burden of her mother. Filial duty was the only thing that took her to visit each week, admittedly never for long. It was bad enough she'd failed to have children, being a failure as a daughter was a final humiliation she couldn't bear—even if there was no woman alive or dead who deserved more to be left alone than.

LP pulled into the driveway of the home Agnes Mayberry had shared with four husbands (consecutively, not all at once, and all deceased in their turn), and now with a sole cat (Puss, sluggish, fat, not dissimilar to the late unlamented Whiskey), and turned off the engine. Hands resting on the steering wheel for the count of fifteen, she steadied her breathing, then got out of the car before retrieving the still-warm baking tray from the back seat.

'Mom?' She knocked and called loudly, even though Agnes wasn't deaf, but she always led with, 'Oh I didn't hear you.' LP opened the door, which was never locked despite all warnings to the contrary. Privately, she suspected no burglar or invader of any kind would stand a chance against her mother's withering stare.

Still no answer. LP moved along the hallway, keeping an eye out for Puss who liked to swipe the unwary from doorways. 'Mom?'

Continued silence and LP knew it was wrong to have that little leap of hope in her heart, to imagine a future where Agnes did not feature except as a name on a headstone. She *knew* it was wrong, something the universe would punish her for, and so wasn't at all surprised when she made it to the open-plan living-dining area and saw her mother. Standing out on the back deck, tall and straight in platforms and a long pink summer dress, blonde hair sprayed so it wouldn't move in a tornado, cigarette in hand, a good inch of ash clinging to its end in sheer defiance of gravity, Agnes surveyed her immaculately kept garden. In her other had was a martini glass, breakfast of champions. LP put the tray onto the kitchen bench, knowing her mother would eat it only after she'd left, lest she had to offer any kind of thanks or compliment.

'Mom,' said LP for the third time and stepped outside. Agnes didn't turn, either at the sound of voice or footstep; even when LP came to stand beside her all she did was blow out a long stream of white as she said, 'Oh, I didn't hear you, Laura Pauline.'

LP cringed at the name.

'Hey, Mom.'

'How's Angie?' Agnes asked, just as she always did; she had a cycle, a plan of attack, nothing changed except maybe the intensity. She never asked how LP was, only Angie, then Kurt, then Whiskey, then Thomas. She'd wax lyrical about Thomas, though she'd seen him once since his birth (hadn't bothered to hold him), and there was no way Angie was going to let the child visit a house the interior of which had a higher air pollution rate than India. As willful and precisely put-together as Agnes was, she wouldn't stop smoking, and even she couldn't prevent the odor from impregnating fabric and walls, staining paint and making toxic clouds against the ceiling.

'She's fine. Kurt's fine. Thomas is fine.'

'What about Whiskey?'

'Gone.'

'What do you mean?'

And it gave LP no end of satisfaction, though she knew it was mean as all hell, to say, 'Gone. As in disappeared. Probably dead. You know how it is.'

'Oh. Poor Kurt. He must be devastated.' Pause. 'After all, that cat was the closest thing he'll ever have to a child.'

LP blinked hard. It didn't matter how often it happened, it didn't matter how regular the digs were, somehow Agnes always found a new way to slip the knife in. It wasn't unusual for LP to spend more time cooking and grooming than in her mother's house. 'Okay, Mom. Have a good day.'

Agnes didn't bother to reply.

LP reached the front door and paused. Through the doorway into the room on her right was her mother's bed with its saffron-colored comforter and mountain of pillows and cushions in various shades of purple. On the mound, like an emperor, lay Puss. He made those angry little sounds in his sleep, tail twitching, and one back foot spasmed as though he were scratching the hell out of someone.

LP stared at the animal.

She stared at Puss for a long while.

She was still staring, wondering if she had time to find the cat box Agnes kept for trips to the vet, when she heard the sound of her mother's heels on the floor. A pause, then very softly, 'Laura Pauline?'

LP left as quietly as she could, feeling a band of tightness settling around her head.

The headache was almost gone by the time Angie drove up at seven-thirty the next morning, just as Kurt was backing out of the driveway; they exchanged good-natured waves. LP watched as Angie got Thomas from the car and the big bag that contained food and formula, fresh nappies and changes of clothes, hopefully enough for an six-month-old for a day, but who know what might happen even though he was less mobile at this stage. Boys attracted muck, in LP's experience (she tried not to think about the amount of filth adhering to the kid in the woods, what that might mean), but she just smiled when she opened the door, as if she hadn't forgotten babysitting or movie night. As if she hadn't spent breakfast trying to figure out where she was going to get more cats, answering Kurt's chatter with a sequence of *uh huhs, yeahs, maybes, whatever you want honeys.*

'Didn't find anything,' said Angie as she entered the kitchen, blue onesie-clad Thomas on her left hip, bag over her right shoulder.

'Huh?'

'Children. Missing children,' explained her friend, managing the impressive maneuver of dumping the bag on the table and handing off the snoozing child to LP at the same time. 'None that stayed missing anyway. How's your story going?'

'Oh. Slow. You know, takes me a while to get going. And this is something different to my normal hobbies, so even slower than usual.' LP adjusted the slightly damp Thomas so his face nestled into the side of her neck and his breath was warm and soft against her skin. Made her heart clench, not in a way that was good or warm, though.

'Well, don't you worry, LP, I've got faith in you. I reckon you can spin a great tale. Don't they say everyone's got a book in them?'

LP smiled vaguely, mind elsewhere. The kid had had three fat, four-legged meals, and LP was running out of places to go. The women at the shelters would notice if she went back too soon, and the cats that lived in the dumpsters behind the Safeway were too leery of humans to come near her no matter what she held in her hand. Anyway, they were too thin, too nervous, and she couldn't imagine them snoozing their day away until the kid turned up. And Puss, though tempting, wasn't an option because it would mean returning to Agnes' house before she absolutely had to.

'Well, I'd better get going, don't want to be late.' Angie gave LP a quick buss on the cheek, placed a firmer one on her son's forehead. 'I'll pick you up this afternoon about five-thirty.'

'Sounds good. Drive safe.'

LP glanced out the kitchen window, while Thomas snuffled and farted in her arms. She had no bait today, nothing to attract the kid; no lunch all tied up and waiting to lure it out of the woods. She wouldn't see it until the next cat. Thomas stirred, his little fists beginning to flail; he farted again and it sounded wet. Thoughts of cats would have to wait until tomorrow. LP wrinkled her nose; she knew when something took priority.

Thomas was fractious and demanding most of the morning, which he usually wasn't but LP normally wasn't quite so distracted by her own thoughts. Usually she played with him and enjoyed his company as much as she was capable, but today just wasn't that sort of day, so it was a relief to put him down in the cradle in the spare bedroom upstairs after lunch. He went to sleep quick, too, like he was just waiting for the whole experience to be over and slumbering through it was the best option he could come up with.

Back downstairs, LP collected the laundry from the washer. She carefully closed the back door behind her—a habit from the days of Whiskey when she kept him out of the house during the day until Kurt returned from work and let the animal in—as she went to the washing line.

While she was pegging up socks and underpants, work shirts and jeans, bras and dresses, LP daydreamed. She'd got a vision board in her head, did LP, where she pinned all the things she wanted in the order she thought they should be. Her mother was fond of saying that *LP don't think things through*, which wasn't entirely true, but not entirely unfair either. LP did think a lot, but what she didn't get was all the angles. She *thought* she did, but she had a tendency, not uncommon for sure, to check only the angles that supported what she wanted. So LP's plans tended to be like fishing nets with overly large holes in them, not strong enough to stand against anything that didn't want to be caught.

By now, LP had a concept, pretty much fully formed, of her endgame. She always had an 'ideal' of that no matter what hobby she took on, and maybe that was why she wasn't really thinking straight about this project. She could see her and the kid (clean and neat and tidy) and Kurt walking down the street together, doing the groceries, going for ice cream, all sitting on a blanket at Kurt's company picnic, just like the other families with their baskets and plates and cups and coleslaw.

No more pitying looks, no more whispers behind hands, no one telling her she'd best get a hurry on before her 'use-by date', no one dumping babies into her lap like they were doing her and her barren womb a favor.

LP was smiling by the time she'd done with the washing. She hitched the basket on her hip, walked back to the house and its open back door with a swinging gait. As soon as she got inside she smelled it. Raw and fetid, a sewer stink. It made her eyes water. She blinked, wondering for a moment and then recalled Thomas. He must need changing again. What the hell had Angie been feeding him?

Unhurried, she put the laundry basket on the couch—the sun was warm and the breeze high, she'd need it again soon—and took the stairs. Halfway up, she seemed to hear a door closing but she knew she'd already shut it when she came in, so she must be imagining things. Maybe it was just the wind rattling it in its frame.

She took two steps into the spare room before she knew

something wasn't right. Normally, she could hear Thomas breathing—he was a snuffler, a snorer, even this young—but there was no sound from the crib. Two more steps, three more, four, and there it was: the empty cradle.

LP was frozen, stunned, bewildered. All those things and more, everything you might feel if you were hit in the head with a brick or a length of wood and not quite knocked unconscious. Stupid. She picked at the blanket and sheet, the pillow, the mattress, the plastic lining, everything, just in case the child had managed to secrete himself somewhere in the small rectangle of space and her eyes had failed her.

She turned on the spot, more than once, then propelled herself out of the room and down the stairs. In the kitchen was the phone, hanging on the wall, and she stumbled getting there. LP almost pulled the handset away from its moorings, held her fingers over the keypad, about to pick out those three numbers, the numbers that would get the cops, would tell Angie far too soon that somehow LP had let her down ... and LP paused, stared. The 9-1-1 keys seemed to glow and burn brighter than the others.

Slowly she looked away, seeking inspiration. Where could he have gone, this baby boy? Sleepwalking, sleepcrawling ...

LP was staring out the kitchen window now, staring, staring, staring, paralysed so only her eyes shifted.

And shift they did as they caught a movement, just as they did a week ago, but this time not slow or cautious or nervous. No. Quick, quick, quick, delighted and wicked and so terribly cruel as the kid, matted hair, filthy skin, long talons, paused at the edge of the woods, a blue-clad bundle in its arms, then scampered off into the trees and shrubs and long grass.

RUN, RABBIT

Rabbit has been running from the Queen for so long he's almost forgotten what he did.

Almost.

Such a small indiscretion, really. Just a teensy-tiny step out of line, really. On this side of the worlds a rabbit's foot is considered lucky, but he's sure folk would rethink that if they knew his many travails and trials. Missteps. He wiggles toes, all seven of them; inside the big black boots he's obliged to wear here, he seems to still feel the one that's missing. Feels the absence of the left little one; it doesn't upset his balance too much anymore. Besides, there was so much to adapt to when he fled, it was the least of his worries. It barely registered beyond the pain when it was taken off, the portal closing its teeth a little too soon, a little too late.

I'm late, I'm late, I'm late.

Rabbit looks around. The place is dimly lit, darkly decorated with striped wallpaper that's trying to make a break for it where wall meets ceiling, and small reddish-orange lanterns sit on sticky laminate tabletops; the leather-buttoned benches are tacky too, both physically and decoratively. He prefers to sit at the bar, likes the stools because they make him feel taller, and he's less likely to be trapped against a table or in a booth. It would have been stylish, he supposes, back in the day, but he can't hazard a guess on precisely when that might have been. Still, he likes it, feels relatively safe there, the stuffy closeness is like the hugging safety of a burrow and there's an earthy smell, too, that almost reminds him of home.

Safe.

Safe'ish.

Not so safe that he doesn't keep glancing at the door whenever it opens. Not so safe that he doesn't already know he can exit quickly through the back office, the kitchen, the tiny men's room, and even tinier Ladies. He knows what to look for in newcomers.

When he'd come through—and come through properly this time, not just jumping over the border then back again like a child on a dare or defying a parent who'd said *This far and no further*—he'd changed. Changed his shape to become like one of the humans. However, he wasn't entirely *solid*, not entirely three-dimensional, but flimsy, weightless as a playing card, feeling as if he turned side-on he might disappear. Not that the humans noticed—such a subtlety was beyond their blunt perceptions—but he knew this strange flatness, lightness, thinness afflicted the Queen's assassins, too. He could pick the bounty hunters from the way they moved, as if fearful a strong wind would carry them away.

'Another?' The barman's voice startles Rabbit, but he does his best not to show it; he smiles at the young man who wears a plain black shirt and matching jeans, no nametag for this is a not a place where names matter. He's handsome in a rough sort of fashion; a good bath and some styling and he'd pass for civilised. Just the sort Rabbit used to like, over on the other side, although he finds he prefers the women here.

'Yes, please,' says Rabbit softly, wistfully, 'same again.'

The barman has large hands, black hairs curl across the backs of his fingers; Rabbit imagines it's on his chest, too, a densely tangled inverted triangle, and thinks of the line of it that will surely travel from his belly button down to the loins. Not very muscular, slender, with ropey veins in his forearms that remind him of the Ace.

Oh, but he's melancholy tonight! Perhaps he should slow down on the whiskey. Perhaps not.

Rabbit watches the barman surreptitiously at first, then realises the youth isn't interested, doesn't care if he's sized up or not; isn't the sort to take offence at being found attractive by another man. He's new here, Rabbit is certain, but he's not sure if he's feeling anything genuine or just an echo of once-upon-a-time.

When the door opens about an hour later, it lets in a rush of cold air and driving rain, and Rabbit tenses. He unhooks his heels from where they've been propped on the lower bars of the stool, ready to run.

It's just a girl.

Then he realises she's got a heart-shaped face, and for a moment his pulse quickens. But she's not a feeble thing, not a fragile card person, not one of the Queen's ladies-in-waiting or hunting hounds or assassins or executioners, or any of the range of professional murderers that woman employs. This girl is solid, walks with a weight on the earth as if she belongs there.

A heart-shaped face, thinks Rabbit almost sadly. Thinks of the card-courtiers with their tattoos to mark out their belonging; that they are *owned*. Thinks of how pretty they were, embracing their servitude yet adding their own twist to it: changing their designs every week (although not the shapes —always hearts) to stay in fashion or ahead of it. He remembers the legions of artists kept to undertake such artwork, the best ones bartered away to the highest bidder for ever-more ridiculous favours (a cake frosted with fairy breath, a dress of sunlight embroidered with moonbeams, a necklace of a child's new teeth).

And he, moving amongst them—hadn't he been a perfectly good courtier and procurer? Obedient and biddable and loyal, bringing new toys as per the Queen's commands. All those fresh amusements and oddities, children from the other side, sometimes to cosset, sometimes to hunt, depending on Her Majesty's whim. And all he'd requested in return was that his foibles be overlooked, his peccadilloes go unpunished. Was that so much to ask?

The last one he'd brought through—just doing what he was told, mind you—that girl! Such trouble; how could he have known? They'd never been like that before. The child was everything the Queen had demanded—a challenge!—yet she'd not been prepared for the consequences.

Hadn't he said? For years. Hadn't he warned? All those times. He'd told her in his most polite, courtly manner, how wild the creatures were no matter that they looked like butter wouldn't melt in their mouths. *So much the better*, the Queen had shrieked. *Adds spice to the day, the hunt, the night*! And so it had, though more than anyone could have expected. It took ages to put the kingdom back together again, to re-establish order. And in the wreckage, all of Rabbit's sins were brought to light.

'Do you mind if I sit here?' A voice at his elbow—*what a stupid phrase*, thinks Rabbit—pulls him back. Not the barman this time, though he's gone and refilled the glass again at some point without asking. Rabbit could afford better booze; he makes good money trafficking just the way he did in the other world, but there's something louche about the cheap hooch that appeals.

He looks at the girl—woman really, though young, youngish—a little blearily. Green eyes, muddy brown hair, unkempt eyebrows that are almost a single entity, freckles sprinkled across a nose that's been broken and healed not as well as it might, and the trace of a scar on the right cheek, a fine raised line old enough to have turned white. Perfect teeth, though, and pretty mouth. Her dress is brown, a strange sack of a thing, some kind of coarse linen with a wide deep pocket across the belly, almost like a pouch; perhaps something so haute couture that it doesn't need to worry about being pretty. Comfortable in its ugliness.

Rabbit doesn't know enough about fashion to make an informed decision. He only knows he misses his stiff collar, starched shirt and tidy waistcoat. And the gold watch, which was the first thing he sold off when he came through, the only thing of value he managed to bring, and something he misses like a limb (even more than the toe). Something he's never been able to find again, no matter how many pawn shops he visits. He thinks regretfully of the treasure rooms of Wonderland, all the gold coins and gemstones stamped with the head of the Queen, their eyes following you everywhere. Then again, the idea of carrying those around ... might they not act as spies? As beacons for Her Majesty's assassins? Something that would help the hunters find him?

'Is it alright? If I sit here? I shan't bother you, only I don't like the booths, they always feel like a trap!' She giggles and the sound is infectious. Rabbit laughs too in spite of himself.

The girl-woman is nothing like his type, the female type at least. He prefers them more matronly and wonders if he still yearns for the aloofness of the Queen, the untouchableness of her, and the mysteries hidden forever beneath her voluminous skirts. But the laughter is like a sudden drug, a drink from a quick silver stream, a ray of sunshine breaking through clouds.

'Of course,' he says with rusty grace, a shyness not

common to him. Rabbit ponders that—usually he's *smooth*. Usually, he doesn't have to try too hard; he's short but pretty with thick white-blond hair, pert nose, rosebud mouth, and muscular body—he's going soft around the belly, beneath the chin, but he does okay, can still attract women to his bed and children to points of sale. He's fine for now.

The girl smiles, no idea of what's going on in Rabbit's head. She offers her hand, which bears many healed scars, fresh scratches. She notices his gaze and says, 'I'm Pleasance and I work as a gardener.' By way of explanation she adds darkly, 'Roses.'

'Ah. I'm Ned.' *Tonight* he is Ned; he has a range of identities, different ones in each city he inhabits. 'May I buy you a drink, Pleasance?'

He assumes this is what she wants. She could have sat anywhere, there are plenty of vacant stools, but she came to him. His nerves are soothed, his confidence firms. *She wants.*

'Why yes you may, Ned.' She leans close, maintains eye contact. 'The cheaper, the better.'

He laughs in surprise.

'A place like this requires cheap booze,' Pleasance says, eyeing the faded velvet wallpaper, and Rabbit can't help but smile with delight.

They chat and flirt and laugh. Rabbit talks about his import-export business but doesn't mention the true nature of the goods. Pleasance confesses that while she loves gardening, she does hate the roses; they're beautiful but treacherous, not to be trusted. They move closer and closer without seeming to do so, and at some point Rabbit realises their arms and hips are touching and he can't think how long they've been like that. He can feel her every breath, every tremble, every giggle shivering through her. She smells like some exotic blend of tea.

It's almost an hour before he notices something strange about the pocket of her ugly dress. He looks down, cocks his head and watches. Every few seconds there's a jerk, a twitch, in the right-hand corner, sometimes it bumps against his thigh; a small rhythmic pulse, like a frog in a sock. Pleasance, reaching for yet another drink courtesy of the barman, sees the direction of his gaze and follows it.

She smiles suggestively and says, 'Do you want to see what I've got?'

He's nodding when the door opens again and the rain and wind blow carry in far too easily three thin men. Rabbit knows them immediately for what they are; with barely a thought he grabs the girl's hand and yanks her from her stool. She doesn't fight but follows, crouching down as he does so they are concealed by the bar. Rabbit's credit card is by the cash register, but he doesn't care. It's one of many in an identity he'll easily discard; there are more pieces of plastic in his wallet. They make it into the Ladies, and soon Rabbit is offering his interlocked hands so Pleasance can use them as a step and slip out of the small window. He watches her backside wiggle and is momentarily distracted from his panic.

In the alley, they lurch then run like naughty children, fingers entwined. Perhaps Pleasance thinks it a game; they've had a lot to drink and Rabbit knows that inhibitions and caution are the first things to flee in the face of the alcoholic flood. When he detects no sign of pursuit after four blocks, he slows; his lungs are burning. He's out of shape, but the girl isn't puffing, she's laughing that joyous laugh again. She leans against a wall, still holding his hand; he swings in, presses his lips to hers, she responds, curls her arms around him, her hands up to the back of his neck—and then there's a sharp, unconceivable pain and he passes out.

. . .

'Rabbit? Oh, Rabbit? Wake up.'

The voice sing-songs but cuts right through him. His headache is so great that he doesn't pause to consider who might know his true name. His mouth is dry, blood pulses hard in his ears; he feels fractured. The voice comes again, sharper this time, impatient. Rabbit opens his eyes with an effort that's like prising open a window with a crowbar. The light is blinding and he blinks, blinks, blinks until its bite lessens. Until the pain recedes and objects begin to resolve themselves into pieces of furniture: stylish sofas, an architectural coffee table, framed paintings that look suspiciously expensive, light fittings cleverly recessed into the walls, a fireplace with copper screens and blue-orange flames in the hearth licking obscenely at each other. Rabbit tries to move, but he's tied to a chair; beneath his mutilated now-bare feet is a plush rug, Kandinsky-patterned.

He'd have expected to wake—if he woke at all—in some abandoned warehouse in a bad part of town. He'd have expected to be cold and wet and uncomfortable; as it is he's warm and not completely uncomfortable, but he smells very bad indeed. No blood as far as he can tell. Not yet.

His field of vision expands beyond his immediate surroundings. There is an enormous patio outside the sliding glass doors, and a silhouette blocks his view of the Manhattan skyline where dawn is threatening. The outline is blurred at first, then firms up, comes into focus.

A girl.

Pleasance but not.

The girl.

But not as she was, or not most recently.

The girl as he first saw her when he lay in wait; when he first hopped across her path as she curled on the riverbank beside her bookworm sister; hopping and tutting, 'Oh dear!

Oh dear! I shall be late!', knowing that children can't resist either a bunny rabbit or a mystery.

A blue flounced dress with a white apron the pockets of which are trimmed with red, black shiny shoes and white stockings, waves of golden hair held in place with an ebony velvet band. The same outfit, but the girl is taller now, just a little, strangely grown, strangely childlike. The scar on the cheek remains, the bump in the nose; she wears her markings with pride. She's human, she never looked like the playing card people, had the right weight, the right heft to fool him.

'Rabbit,' she says almost tenderly. 'Rabbit, do you remember me?'

'Alice.'

'After all these years! Very good.' She smiles but there's no true mirth in it.

'What are you doing? Here? Now? You escaped. You went back to the other side.'

'Oh, yes, I did, but time moves differently between the worlds, Rabbit, as you well know. When I got home too many years had passed, everyone I'd loved was dead or almost so, their memories crumbled to dust and cobwebs. There was nothing left for me. So, I returned to Wonderland.'

'You destroyed the kingdom,' he says, then runs his tongue along his teeth to see if any are broken. He wasn't hit; perhaps a taser, that would explain how fast he went down, why he lost control of himself, why his brain feels so scattered.

She shakes her head, the golden hair shimmering. 'Disrupted, that's all. An easy thing to rebuild. Anyway, after what *you* did my sins were barely remembered. Besides, your Queen and I found we had a common goal.'

'Alice ...'

'She wasn't happy about you and her son. You should have known better.'

'The Ace. My Ace.'

'Not actually yours, the Queen's lovely boy, her bargaining card, a pristine husband for the King of Spades' daughter, an alliance that might have settled much of the infighting. But you dirtied him up, didn't you? Took that lovely virtuous shine off him.'

'They'd never have found out but for you, never come looking for me at such an inopportune moment if you'd not wreaked such havoc. Wasn't that revenge enough?'

'No,' Alice says quite simply. 'I lost everything. How many other children over the years have you led astray, you shitty little bunny? Why do you deserve compassion when you showed none yourself?'

'Please, Alice.'

The left-hand pocket of her apron judders again and again. She notices him noticing once more, and digs her slender scarred fingers into the fabric depths. 'do you want to see? Do you want to know how I found you?'

He nods reluctantly.

Alice pulls out the end of a golden chain. She keeps pulling, pulling, pulling until his precious lost gold watch is revealed and, hanging from the end of the links, is his severed toe. Still furred, the cut end pink and fleshy as if it had only been removed an hour ago. The thing twitches and jumps, trembles and thumps against the watch casing.

'You left this behind. The Queen was reluctant to let me have it—she's fond of wearing it as a pendant—but I told her that if she parted with it I'd bring back your entire skin and she could do with it what she wanted.'

Rabbit closes his eyes in relief; he'll be dead before he reaches the Queen of Hearts. It won't matter what she does with his corpse. He won't feel it, he won't care.

'But,' says Alice and Rabbit cringes at the glee in her tone. 'But I think she won't mind so terribly if I bring you back alive and in one—well, two—pieces and let her watch while I skin you. I'm a dab hand, nowadays.' There's a moment when it seems she changes, back to her sack-like linen dress, which is now made of fur, the pocket *is* a pouch, something she's harvested from another such as he—how could he not have noticed? 'But sometimes it takes a while. A long while before you die, Rabbit.'

Alice listens to him weep. She wonders if he'll cry as many tears as she did when she was small and lost and so far from home. She doubts it, but she'll do her damnedest to make sure he comes close. She looks at his thick white-blond hair and nods.

He'll make a fine cloak; the Queen will be pleased.

THE THREE BURDENS OF
NEST WYNNE

'Your mother,' Nest's father would say, 'was stolen away by the fairies.'

He'd tell her Aderyn had gone looking for mushrooms perhaps too early one morning or too late one afternoon. Owain wasn't entirely clear, only certain that his wife had been taken through either daylight or twilight gate. Taken to dance in halls beneath the earth, or serve there at great feasts, or as a bride for some prince with pointed ears and a sharp nose; any range of fates. There were also the days, admittedly few and far between, when his mood darkened with drink and he said something entirely different. That Aderyn, true to her name, had become a bird. An owl, like *Blodeuwedd* before her, faithless and fatal, she'd grown feathers and taken to the sky. But sure as sun followed moon, he'd deny having said it in the morning; after a while he stopped drinking and Nest sometimes wonders if it's because even in his state of decay he knew he couldn't trust his own tongue.

For a while Nest had collected owl's feathers, wrapped them with a ribbon and kept them in the pretty box Aunt Ceridwen had given her. On moonlit nights, she lay the feathers out on her bed, ordering them and re-ordering as if she might remake her mother this way. After a few years she lost faith. At almost twenty, there are few things she believes in.

Any road, by the time Nest was old enough to question her father more closely—more insistently without the risk of being sent to bed for being too bold—Owain himself was gone. Not physically, but mentally. He wandered in his thoughts, so that he didn't spend many hours in the cottage nestled into the crook of the hill. 'It's cold out here on the mountainside,' he'd tell his daughter even while she could see him in front of her, firmly settled in the worn old armchair by the hearth that was his favourite spot. The telly had broken several years ago and they'd not bothered to replace it; Nest preferred books, and Owain spent time in his head.

It started in small ways, absentminded ways. He'd not take his lunch when going to the mill. Forget his tools. Forget that his sister had died some years before. It got worse and he'd stay in his pyjamas if left to his own devices, forget to go to work entirely, forget to feed himself. Nowadays, he'll obediently eat whatever Nest puts in front of him, but it wouldn't occur to him to help himself; when he gets hungry he simply mewls until his daughter drops whatever she's doing.

One thing he never forgets, however, is that Aderyn's *gone*.

On occasion he *did* leave the house, slip out the door and wander the valleys and peaks. Once, Owain disappeared for six whole frozen days. Nest all but lost belief in finding him again, but she couldn't deny that spark of relief at the idea of being freed of her watch. Love didn't enter into it: she loved him, of course she did, but she was worn down to the bones of her being looking after him and trying to make enough to keep two bodies and souls together. She'd started taking in mending and ironing when she was thirteen (still going to school, still with hope) the year Aunt Ceridwen died and Owain's slide grew faster. She'd held onto her dreams of going away to university for as long as she could, but nothing good grows in shadow and they withered after a time.

But then off Owain went that morning and it seemed he'd stay gone. Didn't she just get the tiniest flame of anticipation inside her of becoming *something more*? She dared to think how she might manage her leaving, selling the tiny cottage; she even sent away for prospectuses from three universities.

Then on the morning of the seventh day Daffyd Morgan found her father, didn't he? She couldn't help but curse him a little. Daffyd brought him home again, said he'd seen the older man (who was barely over forty) wandering around the fields by the mine that had been worked out fifty years ago. Owain, for once, was strangely silent about where he'd been.

After that Nest began to take in spinning on top of the mending and ironing for extra money, thinking she'd need to set it aside for his care at some point. Some days she loses hours, her eyes on the filaments as if she can see through time, forward and back, as if she's searching for a way out. All her wishes turn into skeins, and she might as well try to spin gold from straw for all the good they do her.

But Aderyn. Aderyn was gone before Nest had anything more than cloudy memories of a narrow pretty face, dark eyes, blacker than black hair, and a red birthmark running up the side of a slender throat; that last doesn't show in photos of her but then she's always facing away. When Nest started school, the other children would tease her, say her mam was a ghost, that *everyone* had seen her whenever something went wrong somewhere. Owain, when he still had the wit to do so, told his daughter not to listen. He swore black and blue that his wife had been taken by the fairies and that any other explanation was sheer idiocy (bird transformations included, apparently): her mother was *not* a ghost.

The talk continued but Nest's soul was that of a cynic

even early in life. There was a lack of consistency in the accounts and wasn't there was always something someone wanted to cover up whenever they made mention of Aderyn? Wherever fault might lie, it could be easily shifted by shaking the spectre of the pale woman in people's faces.

This afternoon Nest's in the tiny sitting room, spinning, when she hears the car coming. Owain's lying down in his bedroom. It takes a few moments for her to return from wherever her mind's been, then she goes to open the door; she waits. She does so because the sound of the engine is different. She knows the calls of all her neighbours' vehicles. She can even recognise the little clockwork chugging of those most tourists drive (not too many of them for there's very little by way of ruined castles or blue plaques, seaside vistas or anything else of interest to be honest).

It's a Mercedes, dark blue, new and shiny. The windows are tinted so Nest can't see inside, but it slows past the gate, seeming to take her in as she leans against the doorframe. The wind picks at her black, black hair as if it could be made even messier; there's a storm in it, the breeze, Nest can smell it, feel it in the pricking of her skin. Then the Merc speeds up and continues on, taking the left turn onto a private road that leads to a metal gate in a high stone wall. Only Pugh House down there, big and mostly empty since the owners died. One month apart, pneumonia both, less a tragedy and more to be expected: they were old and poorly and unpleasant, not given to charity or any great kindness at all. Neither Lord nor Lady but moneyed, and that made them better than everyone else. The fact they'd rather pay someone a pittance to mend their linen and clothes rather than buying new things was a sign of how miserly they were. Nest knew she shouldn't complain as that tendency had helped keep her and Owain in food.

No one seemed to know—not even the housekeeper, who was sister to Nest's neighbour Mrs Parry—whether it was being sold. Not on the open market, certainly no, but perhaps in that mysterious way the rich pass things between themselves, money in exchange for goods and services without anyone having seen the sleight of hand required. But perhaps this expensive car is a sign of someone coming to look at the place where only a housekeeper had been left on guard for the past six months. Or a sign, perhaps, of someone coming home, for the old people had a son who'd gone off to university (and didn't that fill Nest with envy with colour of the hills in spring?). Or a sign, more simply, of someone getting lost and taking the wrong road.

Nest supposed she'd find out soon enough. She had mending to drop up to the house herself. Perhaps she'd do it today, rather than tomorrow.

Mrs Parry saw the Mercedes, attracted just as Nest had been by the unaccustomed engine purr. She'd seen Nest, too, standing in the doorway across the road, hair so dark and long and looking too much like Aderyn for anyone's good. So Mrs Parry isn't surprised when there's a knock at her door a while later, and the girl's on the doorstep, a wicker basket wedged at her hip. The tresses are marginally tidier but not much because the girl, for all her seemingly calm acceptance of her lot in life, always looks a little wild.

'Eirys, would you mind sitting with Da for a bit?' Nest asks. 'He's sleeping and I don't want him to wake alone.'

Mrs Parry juts her chin towards the basket, says unnecessarily, 'Taking up the mending then, *cariad*?'

Nest nods, expression neutral.

'Looks like it might rain.'

Nest pulls at the collar of her weatherproof jacket with her free hand. 'I'll not be long.'

'You look very like your mother, Nest.'

The girl doesn't answer, merely turns and walks off.

Mrs Parry watches her go, keeps watching until she disappears around the bend in the road and into the palisade of trees that line it. The woman can't help but feel the pressure of the lowering sky pressing down. She wishes she could have kept Nest back. But some things will come to pass whether you want them to or not.

Eirys Parry, who's given to reading a lot of mythology (too much according to her far less fanciful sister Elin), once said the girl reminded her of a Norn with her thread and shears, looking for a place to cut the line of someone's life. That some days, the girl looked like she'd be happy to do harm. Not that she could blame Nest, what with all her desires being whisked away before she could even taste them. That girl might have been born in the valley but she wasn't meant to stay in it; forcing her to do so would only make her bitter and strong.

Eirys sighs and closes the door behind her, heads across to the other cottage where a man lies sleeping.

Nest knocks at the door of the big house and hates that it sounds so tentative. She's been here plenty before, when the old people were still alive and haunting the place like dead folk who'd not yet lain themselves down. She knocks again, louder, more aggressively. She hurts her knuckles. There's no sign of the navy Mercedes in the drive.

Elen Lewis, Mrs Parry's sister, answers. She's thinner, not so kind, but she's kept Nest in mending work for the past few years, made sure she's been paid on time, and passed her name on to anyone who's looking for a dab hand with invisible patches and neat stitching. There are different forms of kindness, Nest reminds herself. Mrs Lewis stands aside as if she's been expecting the visit—and honestly, she has—and Nest steps into the foyer. When the old people died she got bolder, started coming to the front instead of the kitchen entry. Mrs Lewis has never said anything, though her eyes narrowed the first few times; the girl persisted and the older woman simply gave up.

'Come through, Nest,' she says, closes the door, and walks towards the kitchen.

The basket is beginning to weigh on Nest, filled as it is with heavy cambric sheets and pillowcases. She puts the burden down on the kitchen table (clean as a whistle, as always), then Elen proceeds to inspect the work, one piece at a time. It might be five minutes or ten until she finds the repair, but the longer it takes the more satisfied she appears. Nest's Aunt Ceridwen taught her how to mend and how to spin, told her when she was little all the tales that might go with those tasks to make them seem magical, interesting. For a while it worked, but most things when taken up as employment become less enchanting with each passing second. On days like this Mrs Lewis reminds her of her aunt, but Nest is confident in her skills.

'Good,' says Elen Lewis at last and goes into the pantry where she keeps the household funds in an old tea tin that Nest's only ever looked into once but never taken anything from—she's no thief—then returns with the paper notes.

Nest cannot help herself: she unfolds the money and checks the amount. Not because of a lack of trust on her part, but because Elen Lewis should know better than to check *her* work by now. The housekeeper waits for the little show to be over, then begins the trek from the kitchen to the front door.

A man is waiting in the entry foyer, presumably the driver of the Mercedes.

He wears dark blue jeans and a green sweater with a white collared shirt beneath; expensive-looking boots that no one in their right mind would think are for hiking. He has thinning red hair and pale blue eyes, high cheekbones; early forties, perhaps, maybe a bit younger. Almost as tall as Owain but much more slender, his shoulders wide but insubstantial as a wire coat-hanger. Thin wrists and long hands stick out a little too far beyond the ends of his sleeves. He's staring at her, but Mrs Lewis doesn't seem inclined to introduce them and Nest finds now that she's not especially curious because he's staring at her like he's seen a ghost.

All Nest feels is the urge to run, because this is the way her father sometimes looks at her when he's just woken from one of his frequent naps. Because it means he's not really seeing *her*.

'Hello.' The man's standing at the bottom of the polished stairs, one hand resting on the newel post that's carved like an owl (for the first time in years, Nest thinks of her collection of feathers, how the magic of them never worked), one foot raised as if he was just about to ascend. His voice is soft and Nest barely hears it because there's a clap of thunder; she wonders if she can get away with ignoring him. Mrs Lewis opens the front door and the rain's coming down in sheets. The wind pushes it sideways and it lashes into the foyer. Then lightning strikes the ground in the garden outside and Mrs Lewis shrieks.

'You can't go home in that, Nest Wynne. Come back to the kitchen and wait.' Elin fights to close the door against the tempest.

'Wynne?' says the man, again so softly that Nest's not sure she's hearing it. But she looks at him, nods curtly.

'Is your mother Aderyn?'

'She was.'

'Was?' He goes even paler, if that's possible.

'Who are you?' she asks bluntly.

'Rhys,' he says, seeming to swallow as he says it. 'Rhys Pugh.'

So, the son of the house.

'I knew you mother,' he says somewhat unnecessarily. 'And your father. He's well?'

'Well enough,' she says, unwilling to offer more.

'Please stay?' he asks.

She looks at him, then at the still-open door Mrs Lewis is battling.

Nest flies over the threshold and out into the weather like a stormbird.

The stories about Aderyn began soon after she'd gone (although there'd been whispers before). There was blame to be laid for ever so many things. Hari Llewellyn lost his way one night, only to find himself teetering on the edge of a cliff, just barely saving himself by the grace of God. Betrys Jones' youngest son went a'wandering one afternoon and was found drowned in a well not three hours later. And when Rhoswen Price's best milker dried up overnight there was simply no explanation for it.

Yet when Hari told his story he didn't mention how much he'd had to drink in the pub that very same evening (for his wife had warned him to stay sober), but said he'd been lured off the path by a pale woman. When Betrys' audience began to drift away from her weeping, her husband's attention wavering from sympathy to angry grief, and the woman who'd wrapped the corpse for burial began to ask why there were marks around the tiny throat, Betrys claimed she too had seen that pale woman in the moment before little Dai disappeared. And when it seemed Rhoswen's oldest daughter might have let the cows wander into a field where belladonna grew while she was otherwise occupied with the butcher's boy, why then she too remembered sight of a pale woman roaming the mists that suddenly sprang up from nowhere on a perfectly clear day.

A slim pale woman with black as black hair who looked terribly like the disappeared Aderyn Wynne.

But Nest's never seen her mother's ghost, and she doesn't see it now as she runs home in the storm. Her head's down and the wind's so powerful—spiteful—it keeps reefing the hood of her weatherproof away, so her hair's soaked and icy rivulets of water run down her neck. She's concentrating on the ground that's so quickly soaked, trying to make sure she doesn't slip and slide. Her eyes are pinned on the rushing streams, on the sudden mud, on the pebbles that might prove treacherous at any moment. So she doesn't see the slim figure keeping step with her, perhaps three metres to her left, the substance of its body being whipped away by the gusts, reforming, almost as grey as the rain.

Ghosts are stirred when folk walk over their grave, when the living come back to disturb them, when there's something amiss needing to be put right. Whey they're sad or lonely or angry.

Nest doesn't see at all.

Mrs Parry fusses when Nest gets home. She's not only wet, but frozen with cold and the latent fear that she'd be struck by lightning. Owain's awake, sitting in his chair by the fire; she's irked that her father is so comfy, so toasty, so undisturbed when she's shaking so hard she can fair hear her bones rattle. Mrs Parry's kindly set the dinner table (for three) and Nest can smell a pot of stew on the stove. She knows it wasn't anything from her pantry, so Eirys has brought it over from her own.

'Da, I met someone today, says he knows you,' Nest says as Mrs Parry rubs at her hair with an enthusiasm that feels like it might take Nest's head off. She doesn't truly know why she tells him, because she sensed even in the foyer that afternoon this wasn't someone her father would like. He looked too *soft*, like he wouldn't get his hands dirty for love or money; Owain, having made his living either hitting things or carving them, would have no interest in such a man. Perhaps it's just a spirit of mischief, light malice, a need to make something move. *Shift*. But tell him she does. 'Rhys Pugh.'

Nothing from the chair.

Above Owain's head she can see the wedding photo on the mantle, the one her aunt would point to: Owain looking too big for his suit (borrowed for the occasion), sheepish but proud, and Aderyn, the waist of her cream guipure lace wedding dress just pushing out too far. 'That's you,' Ceridwen used to say. 'You're the reason for the wedding, you kept her here. She's have been gone but for you. She was going up to London to be a model, she was, and she was so lovely. But you're why she stayed.'

When Nest had said, that one and only time, 'But she didn't stay,' she got a good slap for her trouble. For almost a year she'd sneak into the corner shop and surreptitiously flip through the fashion magazines to see if her mother might be in their pages, just a glimpse of that peerless face. But she gave that up too. She doesn't look at any magazines anymore, not even in the doctor's surgery when she takes Owain in for his check-ups.

She goes on: 'Son of the big house it seems.'

Still nothing. Mrs Parry eases up, whispers *Nest*, steps away to go to the kitchen and check on the stew they can all hear bubbling. Nest glances at Owain and he's so very still. Perhaps he's stopped breathing, there in his comfy chair. 'Says he knew Mam, too.'

And still nothing, so she repeats the man's name, louder and Owain rockets up. Normally, when he's upset, it's a messy kind of thing, like an explosion, directionless and scattergun, but not this time. He's propelled forward, straight at her and before she knows it he's got her sprawled on the little square table, his big hands (they're soft-skinned nowadays) are hard and efficient around her throat. He used to fight, bare-knuckle, stripped to the waist, for prize money; that's where Aderyn first saw him Aunt Ceridwen once said.

But here.

Now.

With the feeling of a dinner plate being crushed beneath her shoulder blades.

Her father's grip means she's having trouble breathing, she can't cry out, can't say 'Dadi' which would surely stop him. From the corner of her eye she can see Mrs Parry reaching from the kitchen, feet frozen, too far away, like she's a woman made of salt who cannot move. So, Nest finds what she can, one of the heavy glass tumblers that used to belong to one grandmother or other and she slams it into the side of Owain's head.

The thing stays intact but it does break his skin and he reels away. Nest doesn't watch him fall, however, because over by the fireplace, in front of the wedding photo, is a woman. She's willowy and tall, with pale skin and dark eyes and long black hair that moves as if there's a breeze shifting the still air of the cottage.

But the thing that really gets Nest's attention is the woman's slender neck. There's no birthmark, not like the one Nest remembers, no. But there's a gash, deep and from it flows a river of blood. Aderyn's hands are clasped in front of her heart as she stares wide-eyed at her daughter.

Then she's gone in a blink.

'Dadi?' croaks Nest. 'Dadi, did you see her?'

But Owain doesn't answer.

Five stitches in Owain's cheek, interminable questions and a cream for the bruises around Nest's throat later and the doctor says it might be time for Owain to be re-housed.

'Like he's an old dog who's bitten the hand that feeds

him!' Mrs Parry's said with great offence, but Nest thinks that's sort of how it is. They leave him in the hospital overnight for observation, and Mrs Parry, who'd driven them into town because Nest couldn't stop shaking, takes them home again. She insists the girl eat something and ladles stew into a bowl, but Nest says it hurts to swallow.

'You take a couple of those sleeping pills the doctor gave you. I'll stay so you're not alone.'

'Eirys, who's Rhys Pugh?' Nest asks as she pushes away the meal.

'Why, he's the son of the old folk. Worked all over the world, he has.' Mrs Parry gets up to bustle off the unwanted dish. 'On second thought, perhaps I'll go home to mine. I'm tired after all the excitement.'

'He said he knew my parents,'

'That he did.' She's turned, leaning over the sink. 'I'll be on my way then.'

'Eirys.' Nest's tone is borderline unfriendly.

Mrs Parry sits back down. She rubs her hands through her grey hair before she meets Nest's gaze. 'There was talk about him and your mother, though she was already married and had you.'

'What sort of talk?'

Mrs Parry just blinks, as if there could be more than one kind of talk in such a situation. Instead she says, 'He left the night your mother disappeared, *cariad*.'

Nest doesn't tell Mrs Parry about the sight of Aderyn by the fireplace, hands clasped, sliced neck, the sight overwriting every blurred memory she had of her mother's birthmark. She doesn't tell her how Rhys looked at her.

In the morning, Nest goes back to the big house.

The landscape looks washed clean after the storm, bright

and intensely green, dew and raindrops (indistinguishable from one another) glitter on everything like gems. It shouldn't be this pretty, Nest thinks, and she doesn't really know what she's going to do. Only knows that she woke from a dreamless sleep with a conviction that she needed to come here as soon as she could.

She's about to step into the grounds proper of Pugh House when she sees the new owner wandering through the garden, coming towards her. He moves slowly, carefully, his long limbs giving him the appearance of a stick insect and she can barely imagine her mother finding this man attractive. Then again, she reminds herself, she didn't know her mother enough to pick her tastes; only that Aderyn was with Owain because Nest was making her belly bulge all unsightly.

She darts away as the thin man gets closer, then hides behind the trees by the roadside. He exits the gate and turns to his left, picking his way along the stone wall for a while before heading up the hard-to-discern path into the hills. They walk for almost an hour, she hanging back, he never looking over his shoulder, only occasionally sagging down to sit on a rock or fallen tree when weariness takes him. She wonders if he's ill or simply soft and out of shape. She wonders what he does for a living, what he studied.

At last, he stops in front of a tiny grey stone hut, slate tiles on the roof, two smallish windows, the whole thing leaning to one side, but mostly intact; its door is hanging on one hinge. Feet planted wide apart, palms against his lower back, he arches. His head moves left and right but she can't see his expression. Her fingers in the jacket pocket touch the handle of the shears she grabbed from the basket before she left, the ones she uses to snip skeins, to cut threads when she's done sewing something together. As Nest watches he puts a hand to the door, which falls to the ground with a crash.

After a moment, Rhys steps inside.

After a moment more, Nest follows.

She stands in the doorway for a few seconds, sees he's got a torch and is shining it around the single room although the light that comes in through the dirty windows is almost enough on its own. There's a bed, two chairs, a table, that's all; everything covered in dust and mould.

'How long?' she asks and he jumps, gives a small shriek. He turns to look at her and his face is a pale moon in the dimness. 'How long?'

'What?'

'How long were you seeing her? Aderyn.' Nest knows she's assuming a lot and she's not giving her mother much credit for taste. Except she can't help think that Aderyn suffered the same sense of being trapped, of having all her chances taken away by someone else. By the weight of a child in her belly and the thin gold band that wrapped around her finger like a chain. And that this man escaped with no consequences at all.

His expression gives him away. 'Not long. Six months. You were very small. She'd bring you here, sometimes, when the aunt wouldn't watch you.'

Nest blinks. Searches her memory for this place, comes up empty. She was three when Aderyn went, surely she could recall something. But there was nothing there, not quite a blank but a blackness perhaps. Like something covered over. She pulls the shears from her pocket without really knowing she's doing it. His eyes grow wide as if he's trying to see more in the gloom, but she can see a sweat break out on his brow even though it's so very cool here.

'She was married. She had me. She had Owain.'

'She was beautiful and she was better than him.'

'You weren't.' Nest takes a step further into the room.

'She was supposed to come with me.'

'When?'

'That night. The night I left for university.' He swallows, realises he's said something wrong, and in a second Nest realises it too.

'She was going to leave me behind.'

He doesn't shake his head or nod, just carries on as if she might forget what he's let loose. 'But she didn't. She didn't come to meet me. I waited as long as I could ...'

'And then you went without checking on her.'

'I thought she'd chosen *him*. You might have been mine,' he says, then amends, 'if I'd met her sooner. You'd be living in a big house, not some hovel.'

Nest bristles. The cottage is small, but it's clean and neat and comfortable. He's doing himself no favours with his casual contempt. She takes five steps into the room and kicks his right knee with her proper hiking boots. Hears the crunch, sees his expression, the hiss of air between his lips as he collapses and tries not to land on the injured leg.

'You could have been my daughter.' He gets this out between clenched teeth as she stands over him.

But Nest knows it's not true. Because she'd never be on her knees like this, weeping and begging. He'd never have forced anyone to weep like this. That's why she's Owain's child. Not this snivelling thing her mother was foolish enough to love. More than that she thinks about his expression when he realised Aderyn was gone. He'd not known. And because she's Owain's child, she knows now what her father did.

She thinks about sticking the shears into this thin man. About unpicking him as his edges until the stuffing slides out. Part of her says *No*, but the other part is leaking where he tore a hole in her with his words. Aderyn would have left her behind. Aderyn would have gone if something else hadn't stopped her. Aderyn went anyway, but it had been easier to bear when it had only seemed against her will.

Nest lifts the shears, brings them down with force.

. . .

Nest's a bit late picking Owain up from the hospital because she had to go home and shower, burn the weatherproof jacket and jeans. No one will ask about them, she doesn't go into town enough and no one pays sufficient attention to comment on her wardrobe. Her father's quiet when she collects him, and the nurses say he's been good all night. That he's still got a lot of the sedatives in him and she must make sure he keeps getting his dose with meals. Nest nods and takes the bottles from them along with the prescriptions. She's holds her father's arm tenderly when she helps him into the car. His balance isn't what it used to be. She holds him as if she still cares and supposes that perhaps she does.

He doesn't say anything, not even *Hello*. Doesn't say anything until she fails to take the turn-off to their out-of-town holding. He mumbles, 'Where we go?' and he sounds like a drunkard though she knows he's not.

'Just a nice drive, Da. Get some fresh air.'

The mine closed half a century ago, there's just the vertical shaft now where once a metal cage plied its way up and down carrying men and ore. The machinery's long gone, and the planks they nailed over the hole to stop anyone falling in are old and rotten, splintered and swollen from the elements above and below. Rain, sleet, snow, baking sun are regular and to be expected, but from beneath? Sometimes a stink will rise up from below ground and seep out between the cracks in the wood. So corrosive that any passing rabbit or fox, or bird flying low enough, might get a whiff and swoon.

All Nest can think of is Rhys' expression when he heard her mother had disappeared. When he'd seen her, Nest, in the doorway of the cottage had he thought it was Aderyn, unchanged? Ah, too late to ask now.

She thinks about Owain, how he cared for her all the years

he could until whatever was eating him away inside got the better of him. He'd never hurt her until last night when she'd pushed. Aderyn must have pushed too, seeing Rhys Pugh behind her husband's back. Ever since Nest saw her mother by the hearth all she can taste is that flood of red as if it's pouring down her own throat instead of Aderyn's. It doesn't matter how much mouthwash she's swilled about, there's just the slick on her tongue and at the back of her throat of hot wet iron.

No, Owain never hurt his daughter. He kept her here though. In this fucking valley with its mountains like walls and locked doors, he lost his mind, didn't he, and with it the key to her escape. Another life, put beyond her reach because she was his child and she loved him and so she stayed.

She pulls over by the side of the road. There's no fence around the defunct mine because it's so far out and closed so long ago no rules said there need to be one. She helps Owain out of the car, steadies him. There were other ways she could have done this, she knows, but sometimes there's really only one way that will satisfy.

'Did you go looking for her, Da? When you went wandering? All those days?'

But Owain says nothing.

'Ah, you knew where you put her once, didn't you? Did you forget though? Sometimes?'

Still no answer.

Nest walks slowly to match her father's stuttering gait. He's smaller now, still tall even with the stoop, but he's lighter, so much less on his bones. Whatever he took from Aderyn he took from himself as well; only his life seeped away far more slowly.

There's a malodorous whiff on the breeze as they get closer to the boarded-up maw. Nest coughs. She makes out a mist above the platform, thinks it's the end of one of the mine's fetid exhalations. But then Owain takes in a sharp breath and she sees what he does.

Her mother waits, hovering above the splintered planks that to Nest's eyes look little more than toothpicks. Aderyn doesn't talk. Even ghostly, she's not managed to mesh her severed windpipe together. She's just watching, eyes gentle, smile sweet. And Owain doesn't stop walking, if anything his pace picks up though it doesn't become any surer.

Nest wonders if he remembers what he did. If he believes the lies he told his daughter, about daylight and twilight gates, about faeries and kidnappings, and faithless women who turn into owls. If he's moving forward because of whatever kind of love he has left for his wife, or because he knows he deserves whatever's coming. When they reach the spot where the planks have lifted a little at the edges, he hesitates. But Aderyn lies beyond it, two steps, three, four, and there's no other way for him to get to her what with the brambles grown up either side; he doesn't want to be torn to shreds, no matter what else might happen. No little pains, not for this.

'Go on, Da.' She nods when he looks at her. 'She's waiting for you.'

And so she is. Aderyn smiles and Owain takes a step forward, the tip of his shoe knocking against a bit of rotten wood. He lifts the foot higher, brings it tentatively down. Nest lets his arm go. He brings the left foot up and forward to rest beside the right. The planks protest beneath him but do not break. Heartened, Owain takes another step, then another, and suddenly he's halfway across the covering and Nest thinks *He might just fucking make it!*

But then there's a groaning, a creaking and a splitting and splintering. The boards break apart as if they're trying not to but really have no choice. And her father doesn't look at her as if she's a traitor, he doesn't look at her at all, but at his wife whose neck is bright red with her own blood because that's what happens when a murderer comes near his victim after she's dead, the blood runs once more to tell the world what he's done.

But there's only Nest to watch and witness, and perhaps she's the only one who needs to be there. Owain is gone in a second that seems longer than it should be. He doesn't cry out. Aderyn waits and Nest thinks it must be all those moments that it takes for her father's body to reach the bottom of the shaft. Then Aderyn floats over to the hole her husband left; she inclines her head at her daughter, then descends like a discarded feather into the depths and darkness of the abandoned mineshaft.

Strangely, Nest is pleased Owain won't be alone.

She's on her knees weeping when a gust of gas billows up. It burns her lungs and she can't rise. But something else happens: she feels a thousand tiny pins prick her skin, she feels new bones burst from her back like spears. She feels herself shrink and shrivel, her eyes going round, her nose and mouth scrinching up and in, tightening. Her feet claw and her hands disappear, shorten.

In the seconds before her mind changes entirely Nest understands, at last, that women don't become birds when they're faithless, but when they're released from burdens they never asked for.

Nest stretches her wings and rises.

POMEGRANATES

They write of me as a willing bride, but I was never that.

Born to sunshine, air and life—Demeter's daughter, I loved the upper world and her works in it. Nothing sweeter to me than walking a field of wheat, the golden ears brushing my palms. One moment, under the open sky. The next, torn away by an old man certain of his godly rights.

No romance, no request; didn't even buy me a drink.

At first, I thought it was only temporary. That my mother would save me. That the gods would object to one god treating the liberty of another with such disdain. But after a while, I remembered the Titans. How Father Zeus came to be our king—and finally I saw *his* hand in the design. Then Mother took so long to find me, and when she did at last ...

Those fucking pomegranate seeds.

They write of me as sweet and kind, a dutiful daughter. Gentle and patient, a good wife. Yet there's only so long that kindness can last, hidden in the darkness; trapped against its will. Although my patience remains impressive.

They shuffle me between them, mother and husband, because I've become a thing to both of them. Not that I was ever anything else to Hades, but once Mother seemed to love me for myself.

Now.

Now I'm the reason she gets to be dramatic at the changing of the seasons. As if she's the one going beneath, out of the sun, down to the depths where there are bones and ghosts and things that hunger for blood and what they used to be. As if she's having to clean up after taking Cerberus for a walk through the Elysian Fields.

They write of me as a queen, but if I cannot choose my own fate, step from shadow into light at my own whim, then how can I ever *truly* be a queen?

There are some advantages. In the early days, to stop my 'sulking', he gave me gifts. Silly shiny things to begin with, but the more I refused to smile, the greater those gifts became. The keys to Tartarus, that lower kingdom where the very gods kept their enemies, their parents—the Titans. The secret names of the rivers so I might shift them in their courses if the mood struck. And finally, command of the dead, equal to his own. Unquestioned. Inviolate.

No backsies.

Ever.

I've wandered every inch of this kingdom, testing its weaknesses, loosening bolts and rattling chains.

The Titans, I've found, can be charmed. A sweet word here, a drop of ichor there, a fleshy treat every so often, and they become willing to listen. Open to negotiation and plots. They love a good plot, the old gods, and if you think I've got resentments, you should see theirs.

My husband's a powerful god, a king; but he's not been paying attention.

Let's see what they write of me next ...

LYRE, LYRE

I can't help but feel a sense of relief, to be honest.

I mean, I know you're not supposed to say things like that, it's meant to be all Oh-what-enduring-love-he-followed-me-into-the-dark-vale-of-death. But, come on. Can't a girl have a rest?

All the sitting around while he played his lyre, and as soon as he finished one tune, the next rolls on. All well and good for a court performance or a day out by the springs, some nice background music. But all the time? From morning to night? Composing, composing, artistic temper tantrum, more composing, and then 'Eurydice, come and listen to this, darling.'

Next, all the nodding and the foot-tapping, the *mmmm, mmmm, mmmm*. 'Oh, it's lovely, sweetheart. No, no, doesn't sound at all like the other one, *completely* different.'

I mean, where's the time for my nymphing?

While I can't recommend getting bitten by a venomous snake in week five of a marriage, I also can't recommend getting married after knowing someone for five days. So, the snake sort of did me a favour. Still, a bit extreme.

Anyway, I descended as is the wont of the dead, came here, settled in, got to know people. Joined a book club. Avoided the musicians. Got comfy.

Without so much as a by-your-leave, there he is again, lyre on his back, mooning about, begging the King and Queen of the Underworld to listen to the song he's written about how sad he is without his wife.

So, I'm trying to hide in the background, hoping to slip away and lay low for a bit, but Hades sees me, doesn't he? Calls me up front for the latest rearrangement of a bunch of chords and some vocal gymnastics. Well, I keep smiling because they get upset when you don't.

While both rulers were moved by his power ballad, agreeing to let me go (thank you very bloody much), I think Persephone caught a glimpse of my expression when it slipped. Might have been the epic eyeroll. Because she was the one who put the condition on the whole endeavour. *Don't look back at your wife until you both step out into the sunlight. Have faith. Obey.*

And I knew he didn't have it in him to keep from doing what he's been specifically told *not* to do. We were together long enough for me to have learned that no sooner were than the words 'Orpheus, don't take that, it's for tomorrow's dinner' out of my mouth, than lo and behold the food would be in his.

Mind you, it was a near thing. There we were, trudging up the rocky path. There's me tiptoeing along behind him, doing my ghostly best not to make a sound (fairly easy, to be frank) and he's up ahead, stoic and filled with the spirit of not-looking-backness.

I thought 'Shit, he's going to make it. For once in his life—'

Then, with the exit in sight, so very close to his goal, he turned around, didn't he?

And I, a look of regret on my face, faded back into the shadows and turned around, trying not to walk away at an insultingly fast pace.

So, there you have it. A relief.

LOOM

Twenty years.

He was away twenty years. The first seventeen were very nice, I must say. Before the suitors decided I must be a rich widow—for surely I was a widow after all that time. But I knew he wasn't dead. The birds sang him home, treacherous creatures, telling me as he came closer, but not what he did on the way.

No. I had my loom for that.

Then the suitors moved in and began to eat and eat and drink and drink and insist and insist that I choose one of them. But every day the birds cooed the location of cunning Odysseus. And every day as I wove, the shroud showed me my husband's adventures, all the things the birds left out; patterns only I could see. Less problematic during the war, but when Ilium's topless towers finally burned and he began his journey home, half-a-hundred goddesses littered his path. And he couldn't help but trip and fall into them.

Twenty years.

Every night I unravelled my work, unstringing my rage with quick fingers. The shroud for which Laertes waited, begun and undone over and over, prolonging the old man's life. An unintended consequence.

Then, at last, he was home. The suitors slaughtered; my poor maids too, hung from a tree like so much dirty linen. And my husband, settled back into *his* life.

Twenty years.

The loom's been sitting in the corner for a while now ... long enough to gather a little dust, but not so long that my eyes have forgotten how to see a pattern, nor have my hands forgotten their movements. Their cleverness, their cunning.

I take up the threads, the shuttle once again.

'What are you weaving, my love?' he asks, passing by on his way to the feasting table. Passing me by for the other things. The new maids, a fresh crop of tiny waists and broad hips, swan necks (snappable). No goddesses these, no immortals to yearn after him forever. Circe, Calypso, I *see* you. He's not that wonderful, you let him go, didn't you? All of you. Sent him back to me and that's something I'll not thank you for.

He *did* get rid of the suitors (leeches)—but for his benefit, not mine. His pride, not my protection.

'A length of fabric, my love, for no one; its purpose as yet undecided.'

'My clever wife.' A heedless hand on my shoulder, alights like a bird on a thin branch, and just as briefly. 'I cannot wait to see what you do.'

'Nor I, my beloved. Nor I.'

Why would anyone think cunning Odysseus, Odysseus the liar, would have a fool for a wife?

STORY NOTES

SAME TIME NEXT YEAR

'Same Time Next Year' was written for Mark Morris's *After Sundown* anthology (Flame Tree Press). One of the stories I've always carried around with me is a US folktale called "Lavender", which I read when I was maybe eight years old. Time changes how you view every story, and makes you a bit grumpy as well. I started thinking about another version of that tale, if it wasn't as sweetly sad as the original.

WIDOWS' WALK

Christopher Golden and Rachel Autumn Deering had asked for a story for their anthology *Hex Life: Wicked New Tales of Witchery*. I'd read an article about the rise of 'Baba Yaga Houses' in Eastern Europe, where widows were starting to live together in apartment buildings. Basically they could live safely, not feel threatened by predatory male residents, and know that someone who would there to help—and would also knock on the door every morning to check that you hadn't died in the night. I loved the idea of a similar bunch of old ladies, actual witches in their later years, who helped keep young girls in danger safe until they could learn to look after themselves. The result is 'Widows' Walk'.

THE WRONG GIRL

'The Wrong Girl' definitely comes from an angry place! It's one of only two stories I've submitted cold in the last few years. It came from watching a male behave in much the same way as the male character in the story. Don't worry, the rest is fiction. It was my first original fiction sale to *Nightmare Magazine* (I've had two previous reprints in there).

A MATTER OF LIGHT

'A Matter of Light' was my first Sherlock Holmes foray, thanks to a request from Charles Prepolec and J. R. Campbell. I was able to bring in the character of Kit Caswell, from my novella *Ripper*, and I think she played well with the Great Detective and the Good Doctor. This story originally appeared in in *Gaslight Gothic: Eerie Tales of Sherlock Holmes*.

WHEN WE FALL, WE FORGET

'When We Fall, We Forget' was inspired by reading about bog bodies, the memory of the first time I ever saw one (in the British Museum), and a trip to Orkney. All mashed up with ideas about fallen angels. Marie O'Regan and Paul Kane took this one for their anthology, *Phantoms*.

NEW WINE

Marie O'Regan and Paul Kane asked (again!) for a story for *Cursed: An Anthology of Dark Fairy Tales*. I've always loved the Angela Carter line about new wine in old bottles and I started to think about setting a version of Bluebeard in the US. I've also been fascinated over the years by how often shoes are left behind, and sometimes used as the basis of a memorial to the lost. All those ideas of losing your way, being grounded, leaving the path, and just stepping out of your life still swirl around in my brain—that's how 'New Wine' came about.

WILDERLING

'Wilderling' is the second story I've sold cold in recent years. It's not a supernatural horror, but a very human one. I was thinking about how people get to the point of no return— how often they're just flirting with the edge of something that they know isn't good for them, and suddenly find they've overstepped. And that the consequences are far more dire than they could have imagined. Thanks to Sean Wallace and Silvia Moreno-Garcia for taking it for *The Dark Magazine*.

RUN, RABBIT

Ellen Datlow asked for an *Alice in Wonderland* story for the *Mad Hatters and March Hares* anthology. This was the first time I'd ever written in that world. 'Run, Rabbit' came out of nowhere as I sat in a B&B in Launceston, Tasmania as rain lashed the windows.

THE THREE BURDENS OF NEST WYNNE

Rosalie Parker and Ray Russell asked for a story to celebrate the thirtieth birthday of Tartarus Press. I'd been thinking about Welsh folklore, women and owls, about being stuck in a life that you didn't ask for, and what you might do to escape. My mother's dad came of Welsh stock, so the story's a nod to that side of the family. 'The Three Burdens of Nest Wynne' appeared in *Tartarus Press at 30*.

NEW TALES

'Pomegranates', 'Lyre, Lyre' and 'Loom' are all new to this collection. They came from the same seeds as the reimaginings of Greek myth that appear in the flash fiction collection *Red New Day*. 'Pomegranates' is an alternative version of the Persephone myth; 'Lyre, Lyre' from the point of view of Eurydice; and 'Loom' looks at how Penelope might also have felt about her husband.

PREVIOUS PUBLISHING CREDITS

Some of the pieces included in this collection were first published elsewhere. Permission and copyright information as follows:

- 'Same Time Next Year', *After Sundown*, Mark Morris (ed.), Flametree Press. Reprint. October 2020.
- 'Widows' Walk', *Hex Life: Wicked New Tales of Witchery*, Christopher Golden and Rachel Autumn Deering (eds.), Titan Books, December 2019.
- 'The Wrong Girl', first appeared online at *Nightmare Magazine*, December 2020 issue.
- 'A Matter of Light', originally appeared in in *Gaslight Gothic: Eerie Tales of Sherlock Holmes*, J. R. Campbell and Charles Prepolec (eds.), Edge SF & F, July 2018.
- 'When We Fall, We Forget', originally appeared in *Phantoms*, Marie O'Regan (ed.), Titan UK/US, October 2018.
- 'New Wine', *Cursed: An Anthology of Dark Fairy Tales*, Marie O'Regan and Paul Kane (eds.), Titan Books, March 2020.
- 'Wilderling', *The Dark Magazine*, Sean Wallace and Silvia Moreno-Garcia (eds.), May 2019.
- 'Run, Rabbit', first appeared in *Mad Hatters and March Hares*, Ellen Datlow (ed.), Tor, December 2017.
- 'The Three Burdens of Nest Wynne', *Tartarus Press at 30*, Rosalie Park (ed.), Tartarus Press, September 2020.
- 'Pomegranates', 'Lyre, Lyre' and 'Loom' are original to this collection.

EPILOGUE - CHAPTER TWO

Carboard boxes littered the hallway in Chuck's cottage on the Academy grounds... Well at least what was left of the school after the Council had their way with it. I stood there, staring at the pile of packed boxes, still unable to believe everything we'd gone through. The fight with the Judge and Slayer sat ripe in my mind, but with each passing day it grew easier to push the memory further aside. I reminded myself of the families who had fought alongside us, who believed in us.

Together with my Wolves and Ava, life was about to start feeling a lot more normal... maybe not too normal, but definitely filled with laughs and less danger.

"Are you slacking off out here?" Ava emerged from the kitchen, carrying another box before dumping it on the pile, the rattle of pots and pans sounding. She plucked the felt-tip marker from behind her ear and jotted down *Kitchen* on the cardboard flap.

"It all kinda feels surreal, you know," I murmured. "But in the best possible way, like it's been so long since I haven't worried about something."

"Well if you want something to worry about, no one has packed the bedroom yet." She grinned.

I arched a brow. "I'm not touching anything in there. That's for you and Chuck."

She turned to me, hands on hips. "What you gonna do now that there's no more school?"

I glanced up, my mouth partly opened, my mind coming up blank. "Aside from being with my guys, I don't know yet."

"You probably just need some time off. I already know what I'll be doing." She smirked so wide, her eyes gleamed.

"Really? What?"

Before she could respond, a low growl came from outside, coupled with the grating scratch of wood.

"What the hell's that?" Ava spun and darted to the front door, me on her heels, my pulse racing. Maybe I'd spoken too soon.

She ripped open the door and on the front step stood Jubba, staring at us with huge dark eyes, his fur muddied and knotted, paws black.

Ava squeaked and bent down, scooping him into her arms. "Jubba! Where have you been my little boy. Oh my god, I've missed you so much." She rocked him side to side in her arms, kissing his head, while his eyes bugged out and he stretched out a paw to me.

I broke out laughing. Ava would love him more than I ever could, and in her loving arms, he'd have the best home.

Chuck rushed into the living room, his thundering foot-steps halting in the doorway. When he spotted Jubba, his breathed easily. "Looks like someone's been hiding in the woods."

"He needs a bath, he's so filthy," Ava cooed and pushed past Chuck toward the bathroom, making baby sounds.

"She almost sounds clucky." I chuckled while Chuck's face fell.

"No, she's not." But he paled as he said the words and glanced over his shoulder at Ava's squeaking voice filling the house.

Chuck spun on his heels and marched down the hallway. "Ava, sweetie, he doesn't need a wash. He's a wild animal. Let him rough it a bit. Here let me take him outside and do some manly things with him. I'll toss him into a tree and show him how to get back down."

He entered the bathroom, but seconds later flew back out, slammed to the wall, drenched and covered in bath suds resembling the marshmallow man.

I burst out laughing.

"Honey badges don't need baths, they lick themselves," he blurted.

"That's a cat!" Ava yelled out, but he marched back in.

"Don't touch Jubba, he only wants me," she slammed the door in his face, and I couldn't stop laughing, my sides hurting so much, but in the best way.

"What's going on out here?" Bond emerged from the bedroom, carrying a box, while Judas and Nero did the same from the living room.

Chuck huffed and marched into his bedroom, while the Wolves just stared at me like I was mad as my laughs turned into crazed exhales of choking sounds.

"Oh shit, I can't stop laughing."

"I don't think I want to know what's going on." Judas joined me in three easy steps, his hands sliding to my hips, drawing me closer. His mouth found mine, stealing my laughs, and I fell into his arms, under his bewitching kiss.

"Is it break time?" Nero blurted. "Cause I want in." He moved to stand behind me, and Bond didn't waste a second to do the same. The four of us together, hands all over me, lips on my neck, my cheek, my mouth. The memory of our time away filled me, and a ripple of excitement kindled between my thighs.

Someone cleared their throat, and I peered up over Judas' shoulder to find Chuck standing in the hallway with an unimpressed expression his face, drying his hair with a towel.

"This is still my home until we leave." He didn't need to say the words, but the Wolves broke away from me and wasted no time heading back to pack.

Ava emerged from the bathroom, Jubba wrapped up in a towel, bundled in her arms. "He's all clean." She set him on the floor, and the little critter emerged from the towel before shaking himself. Then he rushed down the hallway, his nails click clacking, and Chuck's eyes widened.

"He's going for the packed boxes." With him rushing after Jubba, Ava joined me back in the kitchen.

I returned to rolling up the drinking glasses in newspaper before placing them into a box. "When did Chuck get so much stuff in here?"

Ava smirked. *Right.* He did it for Ava.

I pulled open another drawer and something pink and fluffy caught my attention amid the mess of can openers, wooden spoons, ladles. I reached down and picked up the pink handcuffs, dangling them from my index finger. "What is this?" I teased, smirking at Ava just as Chuck stepped into the kitchen doorway, drying his hair with a towel. He froze.

My stomach dropped, his eyes widened as he spotted them, and Ava snatched them from my hand. "You saw nothing," she mumbled.

In that silent moment of awkwardness, Chuck walked backward out of sight, and my face burned up "Shit, why do you leave that stuff in the kitchen drawers?"

"Can't help it. Sometimes thing take place in different rooms, and—"

"Stop." I stuck out my hand, shaking my head. "Don't need to know anything else as I'm already picturing way too much of things that will forever stain my brain."

Ava giggled. "Says the person with three boyfriends!" She stuffed the handcuffs into her back pocket.

"Anyway, you were telling me your plans for the future." I reached for another glass as Ava pulled open the fridge before leaning in and grabbing the juice.

"Had this idea I've been floating around." She unscrewed the lid and gulped down several mouthfuls.

"And that is?"

She lowered the container from her mouth, her mouth twitching. "Wrestling."

"What?" I almost choked on my breath and turned to face her completely. "Like on TV, that kind of wrestling?"

She nodded and drank more of the juice, her eyes still on me, waiting for me tell her it was a great idea. Hell, I had no idea, when I couldn't even work out my own future.

"How's it going to work?" I asked.

"Gonna go on the road, traveling to different events, performing, and becoming a kick ass wrestling star."

"Wow."

Her face dropped. "You think it's terrible idea? Seriously, Mor, I am so good at fighting and I attended years of wrestling at school when I grew up. You can do it with me." She bounced on her toes, clasping the juice bottle to her chest.

I was shaking my head before she finished talking. "Wrestling isn't my thing, but I'll be there to cheer you on at every match."

She lunged at me, her arms locked around my neck, knocking the chair at my side to the floor. "Yes, I'd love that so much."

"If you drip any of that juice on me, I swear, there'll be a wrestling match in here," I teased. "But seriously, I'm so happy for you. Glad you found something to chase."

A loud thump came from the hallway, and we broke apart to find Nesrin standing there, legs wide, hands on hips, dressed in a black leotard and leggings, a red belt cinched in at her waist. She looked like a panther wearing a red ribbon.

"Ta-Da! We doing this bitches!" she announced.

"Who are you meant to be?" Bond barked from down the hall. "The evil version of She-Ra?"

"Go hump a goat," she tossed over her shoulder. "I'm Kitty, the Grenade, and I'm going to blow you to smithereens."

"Did it take you long to come up with that name?" Nero chuckled.

"I love the name," Ava declared loud enough for everyone in the house to hear.

"Where's your outfit?" Nesrin asked, her gaze eyeing Ava, and then mess in the kitchen.

"We're not finished packing yet," I added.

Nesrin groaned loudly and rolled her eyes. "I told Salome we'd swing by her place soon."

"So, all three of you are going into this road wrestling gig?" I asked.

Ava was nodding. "I'm going to be Ruby, the Honey

Trap." She smirked and twirled on the spot. "My outfit will be all golden like honey."

Chuck entered the kitchen and collected Ava into his arms, hugging her from behind. "She's definitely my honey pot." He winked down at her, and she giggled.

I wanted to gag, but it was cute.

"Nesrin, what about calling yourself, The Stapler, as you'll staple everyone to the ground." Bond joined us.

Nesrin rolled her eyes. "Now, that's dorky."

"The Chokeslam," Nero added. "Or Doomfist. Better yet, The Brazilian!"

"Nope, those all suck," she snorted.

"The Aphrodite Panther," Judas suggested as he squeezed into the kitchen, his arm around my waist, drawing me against him.

"That's not too bad." I glanced up to Judas, and he kissed me.

"Nah, sticking with mine. It rocks!" Nesrin murmured. "So, what do we have to do here to hurry this packing?"

"Pick up a broom and start sweeping, Grenade," Chuck muttered.

"So, you joining the group, lover boy?" Nesrin eyed Chuck.

He burst out laughing, the sound like a damn exploding. "Too old for that, but I'll be Ava's training manager."

I loved that they'd found their thing, but I couldn't deny that part of me was a tiny bit jealous, a smidgen left out because I hadn't found what I wanted to do with my future.

"Let's get this finished then," Ava murmured, then in an instant, all of our phones beeped with a message simultaneously.

I flinched and pulled the phone out of my pocket,

staring down at the message from an unknown phone number.

You've been summoned to Anarchy.

We all exchanged glances, and I swallowed hard. "What's going on?"

"Only one way to find out," Chuck declared. "We need to go and now!"

EPILOGUE - CHAPTER THREE

Anarchy stood monstrously tall, somehow looking bigger than before, the sunlight gleaming off its black walls and towers. The place had reawakened, no longer forgotten; maybe it was a location we'd come back to more frequently.

Chuck took the lead with Ava and they headed up the stairs to the front door.

Nesrin in her panther leotard bounced after them, and she made me smile because I could just picture her, Salome and Ava all geared up, wrestling. They were going to kill it, and I'd be their number one fan.

I swept my gaze around the yard, the grounds showing no sign of the battle and flooding that had shaken the grounds, and changed so much for our community. We'd come so close to losing everything and everyone we cared for. But pride flooded me to know so many of us had come together when it counted, and for that... I would forever be grateful.

Behind us, the city lay half destroyed, burned down, but it would be rebuilt bigger than before.

Judas' hand slid over my lower back, urging me forward. "Should we go find out what's going on?"

I nodded. "It is weird that I don't want to?"

"After everything we went through, it's normal. I keep waiting for the next thing to drop into our lap." He laughed and his smile calmed me like it always did, the way the corners of his eyes wrinkled, the love in that shone out had a way of making me forget everything else.

"Just remember," he said. "We're in this together, no matter what it is."

Hand in hand, we climbed the steps, Nero and Bond following us. We entered the great hall. Instead of darkness, light now spilled over the marble floor and columns. The grand staircase almost glittered beneath the sunlight pouring in from the windows, and the heaviness once in this building was now gone.

Dozens of eyes were on us as we sauntered inside, and all the supernatural races were present, looking our way, smiling like they knew something we didn't. Well, they did; nerves were dancing over my flesh. What exactly was going on?

Dad stood by the steps, in conversation with several men I didn't recognize.

"What's Marcus doing here?" Judas murmured near me.

"The Lycan Ancient?" I stared at the tall man with wide eyes, his skin deeply tanned, with a scraggly beard that clung to his face. Near them were two other men who stood with authority. One was Ava's dad, a man that even at his age, was gorgeous, like all Sea Creatures. The fourth man I'd never seen before.

Dad met my gaze from across the room and gave me a

small smile, then clapped loudly to draw everyone's attention. He climbed up a few steps to stand over the crowd.

"Thank you for coming here at such short notice. So much has happened lately that has impacted us all one way or another. Most of the ruling races have Ancients appointed, who are the overruling leader, who holds the power needed to command their race." He paused and glanced down momentarily. "It's with a sad heart that we recently lost Vlad Vasile in battle. He will be missed by all. On his behalf, I've met with three other Ancients, Marcus, the Lycan leader, Llyr from the house of Sea Creatures, and Bael who traveled a long distance to join us, the Panther Ancient."

"Oh," Bond mumbled, and I glanced over to Nesrin who grinned from ear to ear, pride etched on her expression.

Light chatter swept over the crowd at this group of powerful leaders: many of the Ancients weren't seen in public often, let alone together this way.

Dad's voice boomed. "I have consulted with the heads of the races about Vlad's last command."

"Do you know what he's talking about?" Nero whispered.

I shook my head. "Dad hasn't told me anything." Though I already suspected what would take place, and I couldn't be happier for Dad.

"We will rebuild our lives and community once again, and to take us into the future, we need a new breed of Ancient to lead us," Dad continued. "With Vlad's last dying breath, he appointed Morwenna Livingstone in his place."

The crowd broke into loud murmurs, even cheers, and everyone turned toward me.

Every part of me paused, waiting for my brain to catch up. "Wait, what did Dad just say?"

Judas wrapped his arms around my middle, his breath on my ears. "Babe, you just got appointed as the new Vampire Ancient. Fuck, this is huge!"

My Wolves were there, kissing me, Ava grabbed my arm, dragging me through the parting crowd while my brain rattled.

I tried to remember how to speak, totally stunned by the announcement, his words bouncing inside my head. They must have made a mistake, the position belonged to Dad, not me. Never me.

So many people offered their congratulations, their wide smiles, and I wasn't sure where to look. Not when the room spun around me.

"Ava," I mumbled, and she glanced back.

She spun and gave me a huge hug. "Don't look so terrified, geez. Smile a bit, you're a freaking Ancient. Holy crap."

"I-I think they made a mistake."

She pulled back and shook her head. "Nope. This is what you're meant to be, this is your future."

Her words hit like a flashing lightbulb, clearing the fog. She dragged me forward, and stepped aside when I stumbled to the front.

I lifted my gaze to Dad, swearing I saw tears in his eyes. Taking a few steps down, he collected me into his arms. "I couldn't be prouder of you, Mor. This position is made for you."

Tears bubbled in my eyes and fell as I pressed myself against my dad's chest, hugging him, never wanting to let go.

When he finally broke away, he straightened and I

quickly wiped the tears away. With a loud voice, he asked, "Mor, do you accept the position of Ancient, ruling over the Vampires with a caring but strong hand?"

Glancing over the crowd, their smiles beaming, I had no doubt this was the right decision. I turned back, meeting each of the Ancients' gazes, getting their approving nods, and lifted my chin.

Everything was happening so fast, my thoughts reeled, and my rejuvenated heart thumped in my chest. But when I thought back to everything I'd gone through, wanting nothing more than to protect those I love, to end the cruelty, I knew this was the right decision. The floor beneath me gave a slight shiver like even Anarchy agreed.

With a strong voice, I replied, "Yes, I accept my position as Ancient."

Marcus stepped forward. "Give me your hand," he instructed, his voice deep and raspy. When I looked up at him, silver lined his hair and lines scored the edges of his eyes.

I lifted my hand and he slipped a golden ring, thick and encrusted with emeralds onto my middle finger. Just like I'd seen Vlad wear.

"We had it resized," Marcus whispered, his face beaming with joy.

"Thank you."

In a heartbeat, the explosion sounded, and I flinched, terror gripping me. Balloons and streamers fell from the ceiling, and the sound was nothing more than a balloon popping.

Everyone burst into laughter, an upbeat song filtered across the room, and servants in black suits entered carrying silver trays of treats.

"This is your party," Marcus said. "Congratulations."

I shook his hand and he moved into the crowd.

Ava's dad stepped closer, his hands clasping my shoulders, drawing me in as he kissed my cheeks. "No one else was more deserving than you. Thank you for bringing so much cheer to Ava." With a handsome smirk, he stepped past me.

Bael didn't say a word but I hugged him, his large body swallowing me into his embrace. "I've only heard incredible things about you, Mor. I am proud to serve alongside you."

His words rattled me. "You don't even know me." I murmured.

When he stepped back, his dark eyes grew intense, and I suspected he wasn't a man who minced words. "I trust those close to me. And you will be exactly what is needed."

"Thank you. That means the world to me."

With another embrace, he moved to join the party, and my attention fell on Dad who watched me with admiration. Mom was at his side, both of them tearing up.

"Stop crying, or I'll be a blubbering mess."

"Mor, this is everything to us," Mom said, and Dad just couldn't stop his mouth from curling upward.

"So what am I supposed to do first?" I asked, my mind rushing with a million ideas.

"First, we celebrate." Dad turned me around by my shoulders to face the party. "This is for you. Work comes later. Right now, we all need to remember the good times."

In front of me, my Wolves waited, as did Ava and Chuck. Even Nesrin was nearby in her leotard that made me laugh. Having them in my life made me ridiculously happy, and I hurried to be with them.

"I can't believe this is happening," I murmured as they closed in, with kisses and hugs.

Chuck's strong hand looped over my shoulder, drawing

me closer. "Always knew you were destined for huge things."

I pulled free from Chuck. "Couldn't have gotten this far without you."

He winked as Ava grabbed my arm to draw my attention.

"I have questions." She counted on her fingers. "Will you move into the Ancient's mansion? Will your lover boys join you? Can we have sleepovers even if you're now the big honcho on the block?"

"I haven't even thought about any of that yet." I stared at Judas, Bond, and Nero.

"Works for me," Judas finally broke the silence between us, the other two nodding.

And it hit me right then that I was about to move in with my three Wolves. I rocked on my feet, my mouth falling open that so much was happening so fast. "I'd love that so much."

People kept coming over to me, congratulating me, and while it felt surreal, the new role was sinking in fast.

Judas' parents and Marcus moved closer. "Mor, you will make everyone so proud," his dad explained.

"I'm going to try my best."

Marcus nodded and cleared his throat. "You will do well. And Judas, you better listen up and take care of Mor. I'm growing old and tired, and I might be ready to pass on my title too."

Judas broke into a nervous laugh, but Marcus had his focus on my Wolf, intense and serious.

His parents just grinned.

"Now, go have some fun," Marcus commanded. The three of them turned away and I clasped Judas' arm. "Holy crap. Was he saying what I thought he was saying?"

His face paled and nodded.

"Damn, you guys are gonna rule over most of the city, you know that?" Ava blurted, her eyes bugging out with as much shock as I felt.

"Gah," Nesrin howled. "Are you guys just gonna gush all day or can we party already?"

Chuck leaned over and collected another glass of beer from a passing waiter. "I'll party from over here."

Ava glared at him and grabbed his arm, having no plans on letting him leave our sides. She was adorable.

I turned to Nesrin. "Hell, yeah. Let's show them what party animals we can be!"

The seven of us headed to the dance floor as a team, always sticking together.

Giddiness filled me. Yep, I was the luckiest person in the entire world. After everything we'd been through, I never once believed I'd find a way out of the darkness.

But guess I was mistaken.

Happily ever afters did happen, and I'd just become the Queen of my own kingdom.

It feels like we just started the Beautiful Beasts Academy series, plotting our world, setting up the scenes, laughing at so many Kraken jokes...
Writing the last book was a lot of fun as we brought every thread together, and what it told us was that we had a blast writing together.
So this is just the beginning. The Kila Foung team have several series in the works, and you will be blown away when you see them.

Join the Kila Foung Facebook group, and you won't miss a thing.
Thank you for joining us on this journey.
We love you!
Kim and Mila, a.k.a Kila Foung

Seductive mists and a ruined Academy.

No one will escape this Halloween night unsatisfied

One ruin stands in Mor's way of restoring Trick's City.

The one place where it all started...

Bestias Academy.

As workmen descended with sledgehammers in hand a dark, ominous mist appeared to halt them in their tracks.

It's now up to Mor to figure out what the mist is and why it's appeared days before the most important holiday of the year...Halloween.

And she needs the gang to fight the darkness together.

Only this mist wants to claim more than the Academy grounds…

It wants Mor.

And then it wants the City.

Seduction rises and spills through the darkened streets.

Mor and her three gorgeous Wolves are swept up in darkness…and lust.

BRAND NEW!

Cruel eyes. Perfect lips.

I don't want to crave them but I do. They say only the strong will survive.

In my case, the only way might be to shatter my heart.

The Old Gods weren't dead. They were just bored.

They turned that restlessness to those under their control.

And created a game between the Legions.

A game of survival.

A game of wit.

A game where you must kill or be killed.

A game where those who win don't just escape with their life. They get to stand beside the Gods themselves.

Five students are chosen to represent their Deity.

I'm here to stand before Artemis, the Goddess of the Wild Hunt to show her I'm not just capable, but I'm worthy. Only as the trials begins I'm pitted against the Hunters. Four strong warriors Artemis picked herself. They're cruel and more beautiful than I can imagine. But Briar, their leader is determined to not just win. He's determined to take me down. And I don't know why...

Kila Foung is turning up the heat!

Artemis' Divinity is Hunger Games meets The Cruel Prince with a heart-pounding Dark Academy enemies to lovers reverse harem storyline with a strong heroine and four intense and demanding warriors who'll make our heroine question everything, including her own lust.

ABOUT THE AUTHOR

Angela Slatter is the author of the gothic fantasy novels *All the Murmuring Bones*, *The Path of Thorns*, and the forthcoming *The Briar Book of the Dead* (Titan Books), and the supernatural crime novels *Vigil*, *Corpselight* and *Restoration* (Jo Fletcher Books). She's also written twelve short story collections, including *The Girl with No Hands and Other Tales*, *Sourdough and Other Stories*, *The Bitterwood Bible and Other Recountings*, and *A Feast of Sorrows: Stories*, and the novellas, *Of Sorrow and Such*, *Ripper* and *The Bone Lantern*. Her Hellboy Universe collaboration with Mike Mignola, *Castle Full of Blackbirds*, was released in 2022.

Vigil was longlisted for the Dublin Literary Award in 2018, and Angela has won a World Fantasy Award, a British Fantasy Award, a Ditmar, two Australian Shadows Awards and eight Aurealis Awards. *All the Murmuring Bones* was shortlisted for the Queensland Premier's Literary Awards' Book of the Year and the Shirley Jackson Award. Angela's short stories have appeared in Australian, UK and US Best Of anthologies. Her work has been translated into Bulgarian, Dutch, Chinese, Russian, Italian, Spanish, Japanese, Polish,

Hungarian, Turkish, French and Romanian. Film rights have been optioned for her novelette 'Finnegan's Field'.

She has an MA and a PhD in Creative Writing, is a graduate of Clarion South 2009 and the Tin House Summer Writers Workshop 2006, and in 2013 she was awarded one of the inaugural Queensland Writers Fellowships. In 2016 Angela was the Established Writer-in-Residence at the Katharine Susannah Prichard Writers Centre in Perth. She has been awarded career development funding by Arts Queensland, the Copyright Agency and the Australia Council for the Arts.

Find her online at www.angelaslatter.com

facebook.com/angelaslatterauthor

twitter.com/AngelaSlatter

instagram.com/angelaslatter

amazon.com/Angela-Slatter/e/B005QQ9FOA

ALSO BY ANGELA SLATTER

SOURDOUGH STORIES

Sourdough & Other Stories

The Bitterwood Bible & Other Recountings

The Tallow Wife & Other Stories

Of Sorrow & Such

All the Murmuring Bones as A.G. Slatter

The Path of Thorns as A.G. Slatter

The Bone Lantern (Forthcoming)

The Briar Book of the Dead as A.G. Slatter (Forthcoming)

COLLECTIONS

The Girl With No Hands & Other Tales

Midnight & Moonshine (with Lisa L. Hannett)

The Female Factory (with Lisa L. Hannett)

Black Winged Angels

Winter Children & Other Chilling Tales

A Feast Of Sorrows: Stories

The Heart Is a Mirror For Sinners & Other Stories

Red New Day & Other Microfictions

VERITY FASSBINDER

Vigil

Corpselight

Restoration

COMIC BOOKS

Castle Full of Blackbirds (with Mike Mignola)

NON-FICTION

You Are Not Your Writing & Other Sage Advice

What To Do When You Don't Have A Book Coming Out & Yet
More Sage Advice

www.ingramcontent.com/pod-product-compliance
Lightning Source LLC
Chambersburg PA
CBHW020819190726
48285CB00006B/2338